ULF'S TALE

JOHN BROUGHTON

Special thanks go to my dear friend John Bentley for his steadfast and indefatigable support. His proofreading and suggestions have made an invaluable contribution to
Ulf's Tale.

1

OXFORDSHIRE, EARLY NOVEMBER 1002 AD

Treachery gains more purchase on the imagination when people are at war. The fateful year 1000 had come and the wretched, ever-worsening state of the world provided manifest evidence to support the view that the Last Days were in progress. Venerable bishops added their voices to those of wandering scoundrels who intoned the End of Days: *'War shall come upon war, tribulation upon tribulation, famine upon famine, nation upon nation and yet the bridegroom does not come.'*

In these circumstances England found itself beset by Viking attacks for twenty and more years, failing to resist incursions, its kingship paralysed by poor leadership and treachery.

Aethelred II wore the crown, enthroned as a boy king since his supporters murdered his half-brother, Edward the Martyr. Little wonder that sea raiders swarmed to England for rich pickings.

Betrayal! Surely the vilest such act is to murder hostages bound by a sacred oath of protection. That fate might have been mine at the beginning of November 1002. Back then, I was a mere boy of nine, weak and trembling. I know it's difficult to imagine as I stand in manhood before you with iron-hard muscles tempered in battle.

Many a warrior has quailed and fallen like a felled oak under the mighty blows of my battle-axe.

Let me take you through the events of many years ago. With treason rife you never knew who you could trust, but the ignoble vice can work both ways. So it was that a Saxon thegn who, betraying his lord, came to Eilaf, my brother, to warn us of Aethelred's infamy. He advised of the imminent edict to eradicate Danes from the land. The politics behind this decision meant nothing to us in our youthful naivety but we understood the warning that men with sharp blades were coming to slay the King's hostages.

Eilaf, four winters my senior, came to our bedchamber, his long blond hair combed down and plaited like a maid. Thus he appeared to my sleepy eyes, dressed in woman's garb.

"Ulf! wake up!" he shook and the agitation on his face snapped me out of drowsiness.

"Eilaf! Why–"

"Hush! Make haste and dress. They are coming to slay us."

"Who–"

My brother seized me by the arm to haul me, stumbling, out of bed.

"Dress! And be quick."

Ignoring my frantic questions as I tugged on my tunic, breeches, belt and shoes, I managed to gain Eilaf's attention only when I confessed my fear.

"Remember," he hissed, "you are the son of Thorgils Sprakalägg; courage is in your blood."

That was the point; I did not wish to study my blood pooling on the floor before me.

"This way!" ordered my quick-thinking brother, "They mustn't find us here."

If I am alive today, it is thanks to Eilaf. At nine winters of age, I was as near defenceless as a babe. He led on by candlelight into a large chamber. There, he took me to a wicker linen chest, and made me clamber inside before lowering the lid.

"Keep as silent as a night owl!" he whispered, but I needed no telling. "Stay there until I come for you! Do not move!"

I watched him sway across the room, imitating a girl's gait, in the dim light cast by the smoky wall-mounted tapers. My forefinger bored at the willow weave of the linen chest to widen a gap sufficient to let me keep an eye on the door and the space between it and me. I recall being warm and cosy, the folded sheets and coverings made a comfortable bed. The thick air induced sleep and, barely awake, I began to slip back towards slumber.

My somnolence did not last long before voices jerked me to alertness. A fearsome bristling figure with a sword brandished in one hand, and the other clasped around the wrist of a servant girl, strode into the room. I needed the toilet but knew I dared not move.

"Let me go!" cried the servant.

I knew the voice, my heart thumped twice as fast. It was no maid but my brother, Eilaf.

"Do not play me for a fool child," the gruff voice of the intruder terrified me, "you know what can happen to a pretty little bauble like you, don't you?"

He hauled Eilaf to him, pressed his body into his dress and planted a kiss on his lips. Eilaf struggled like a wildcat but the man only laughed and said, "Now, sweetness, you take me to your mistress, Gunnhild, and you need fear no more. Understand?"

"Release the child!"

My eye switched to the door where, in shadow, stood the noble figure of our distant cousin who, had she survived, would also one day have become my aunt by marriage. The swishing of her gown as she passed my hiding place remains in my memory. The horror of the moment lingers too. Although I was young, I had the certainty that the beautiful Gunnhild was walking to her death. I saw Eilaf race out of the room, heard the groan of Gunnhild, saw her sway and stagger before collapsing on the floor. A crimson lake formed around her body, flowing from a gaping gash in her throat. I can describe no more because tears blurred my vision and terror seized my galloping heart. I had to rely on my hearing.

"What do you mean to do with yon needle, my bonny?" the murderer asked. "It would be a shame to skewer a lovely Saxon maid with my trusty blade. You are a spirited wench, I'll give you that. Come, you can lead me to the bedchamber of the Danish whelps."

I could not bring myself to look at the grisly sight on the floor so when my brother led away the killer, I closed my eyes tightly. Eilaf must have returned with a hand-seax to try to save Gunnhild but how could he? A boy of thirteen winters against a Saxon warrior armed with a sword? Eilaf at that age possessed all the courage he would later display in warfare. Realising he was too late to help Gunnhild, he used his wits to overcome adversity. He led the slaughterer to our bedchamber, which, of course, was empty.

"Ah, the birds have flown!"

He flung Eilaf on the bed and my brother feared the worst, but the man did not wish to satisfy his lust.

"I must seek out the Danish whelps..." and with that he left my trembling brother to curl up on the bed. He waited, listening and fearing the return of the brute, but it never happened. Instead, he told me, the night dragged on until the first light of morning, when a scream averted him of the finding of poor Gunnhild. From my refuge, I saw the servant find the body. Her shriek assailed my eardrums as she was but three paces from my hiding place. Soon, the room was full of people. Among them I saw the lord of the hall, a thegn whose name I never learned. I remember him railing against everyone and against fate itself that he had been placed in the position of failing to protect his noble hostage, the sister of the Danish King, Sweyn Fork-beard. Hearing his ranting, I knew he feared the wrath of King Aethelred, but because of my youth, I was confused. Why would the King be angry if he himself had sent the killer?

They took the body to a chapel and servants mopped the floor. It seemed forever before Eilaf, dressed in his own clothes, came for me. When the room was empty but for us, he opened the chest and helped me out. My legs buckled from stiffness and lack of movement but soon, after rubbing them, I was able to walk.

"Come, Ulf, we must flee this place. We cannot stay here."

"But he...the...the killer, he's gone."

"They'll be back. Their work is but half done."

I needed no more convincing. So we sneaked out of the hall that had been our home for the last two years.

"Are we going back to Sweden?"

"When we can obtain passage. For now, we must make our way to those who can help us."

"And where are they?"

"In a town near here, called Oxford. Come on!"

"I'm hungry."

"Think of saving your life first and of filling your stomach later, little brother."

"I'm not little!"

"No, you're a mighty Viking warrior!"

I flushed with anger and my frightened eyes stared around the great hall where our furtive creeping had brought us. I think it was then that I decided to repay the Saxons for the murder of Gunnhild and for causing the ursine grip of fear that threatened to crush the last of my resolve. We slunk in the shadows of the dim hall along the wall towards the doorway. The acrid smell of charred logs from the hearth pricked at my nose and I stifled a sneeze.

"Hush!" Eilaf whispered.

When no-one could see us, he slipped out of the hall and I followed as fast as I could. Eilaf tugged me down behind a water trough.

"Until we get to Oxford, we must keep out of sight and treat everyone as enemies, right?"

What I remember most of the march to Oxford was the gnawing at my stomach. I let Eilaf take control. He was older and wiser than me and I'd always looked up to him. To give him his due, he had thought of everything. He took money from Gunnhild's room and found a woodland stream on our way to the town. The fresh water went some way to making me feel better. I did not complain during our tiring journey, for Eilaf had enough worries, I understood that much.

When we strolled into the town I felt all eyes upon me and, warned by Eilaf to consider the Saxons as enemies, I felt as though all the world threatened us. I need not have worried. News of the King's edict would not arrive for another two days. Eilaf observed everything and everybody carefully until he heard two men speaking our language. Not Swedish but near enough, sufficient to understand and be understood. These two were Danes and Eilaf learned from them where in town we might eat in Danish company. At last, my stomach was satisfied and we had found lodgings. Gunnhild's purse proved to be well stocked with silver coins so we had no worries for our bodily needs.

It was clear to Eilaf that we were not out of peril. To me, all that mattered was that I was warm and fed but I did recognise the need to find a way back home to mother and father. Eilaf set about the task of seeking passage. It was not straightforward because our presence among the Danish artisans of Oxford had elicited much curiosity.

For this reason, a man named Haldor, a tall, shaggy-bearded, stern-looking fellow sought us out at our inn. He claimed to be the elder or headman of the Danes in Oxford.

"Tell me how you come to be here in Oxford. Who are you exactly?" His suspicious eyes roamed over the two of us. Our fine clothes marked us out as superior to the common folk. At first, I left the talking to my brother.

"We are Eilaf and Ulf Thorgilsson. We were held by King Aethelred as hostages. They came in the night and slew Gunnhild."

"What? They slew King Sweyn's sister?"

"Ay," we nodded together.

Haldor looked from one to the other of us, "And you saw the murder?"

I nodded again.

"By Odin, the oath-breakers will pay for this in blood and fire!"

Eilaf caught Haldor's eye as he rose to leave.

"What is it?"

"The informant who saved us told me that King Aethelred has issued a decree that all Danes must be eradicated from the land. I thought I'd better warn you." The greybeard laid a hand on Eilaf's shoulder, "Did he, by Thor? My people will be grateful to you. '*A man who is forewarned is forearmed*' " he quoted. "I will send a man to you who may help find you a ship. For now, my thanks, we will meet again."

But we never did. They killed him.

2

OXFORD, NOVEMBER 13 1002 AD

T he man Haldor sent to the inn with information about a ship told Eilaf that to cross straight to Sweden was impossible. We would have to sail to Denmark first and thence travel onward to our homeland. I liked this bluff Dane, named Niels. He toiled as a leather worker for a business run by his wife-brother. Seeing Eilaf carried a hand-seax thrust behind his belt without a sheath, he measured the blade with his thumb from joint to nail and promised to make him one.

"I'll bring you something too, young man," he said with a grin, while he ruffled my hair.

Niels's gift turned out to be a pouch for my belt. Well crafted with neat stitching, it bore a stylised raven's head on the flap. I use it to this day, although it bears signs of age. Inside, within one of the three compartments, nestled a silver coin. I made to hand the money to Niels who shook his head and said, "You know, Ulf, it's tradition to place a coin in any purse, pouch or bag gifted. So it's yours. Spend it well."

Niels would accompany us downriver to where his cousin, taking a rest between trading trips to Denmark, had a boat moored. His ship

8

lay tied up at a wharf a couple of hours from Oxford, where the River Thames flowed more deeply. Maybe we could sail with him on his next voyage.

The three of us were setting off when a short, bandy-legged man with a deep voice called after Niels to halt. His expression revealed his uncontrollable anxiety and his speech became undecipherable as he gabbled some kind of warning. From Niels's reaction, something terribly amiss had occurred.

"Boys," he said, turning to us, "I cannot depart now. My sister and her husband are in danger. The Saxons wield arms and are slaughtering our people. Stay here inside the inn and if anyone comes, hide! I must go to help my family. Wait in your room for me and do *not* set foot outside."

I did not want to leave Niels and dashed after him but he snapped at me that he had enough to worry about without having to protect me too. He cuffed me around the ear and sent me packing. With reluctance and a sense of foreboding, I went back to the tavern where Eilaf berated me for my foolishness.

Inside the inn, the first sounds of trouble drifted through our open window. The clash of steel soon outdid the angry, frightened shouts, running feet, barking dogs and women's screams. Fighting had broken out nearby. Curious, we peered out, on our hands and knees, taking care not to be seen by anyone from below. Not that any action happened in our street except for people hurrying past, clutching weapons – cudgels, pitchforks or metal bars.

No way for us to know what they intended, or where they were heading.

"What shall we do?" I asked my brother.

"Nothing."

"But we can't stay here forever. What if Niels doesn't come back?"

"He will," Eilaf's certainty reassured me. I think at that age I would have believed anything my brother said.

So, it came as no surprise to me when Niels returned. His blond hair was matted with dried blood and his pale green tunic spattered with crimson stains.

"Are you hurt?" Eilaf enquired.

"My head's thumping, but I've been lucky."

Something ominous about his tone made me fearful, and I'll never forget the haunted look in his eyes.

Eilaf hushed me with a shake of his head when I opened my mouth to ask questions. Only then did I notice Niels bore an axe hanging from his belt.

"We'd best be on our way," the leather-worker said. "Let's see if the innkeeper will sell us some food for the road. We've only two hours to cover but with these troubles..." He seemed reluctant to complete his thought.

Before leaving the safety of the inn, Niels slipped outside to check the situation. Back at once, he urged us to hurry into the street.

"This way, look lively!"

Eilaf and I had to run to keep up with Niels's long strides.

"The sooner we're out of Oxford, the better."

I thought of Gunnhild, then of the blood smeared on Niels's tunic, and shuddered. Had I known what was happening in the town I would have outstripped a running deer. I had no inkling about the violence until Niels called a halt by a stream in some woodland after we left the road. There we quenched our thirst, and lunched on the bread and cheese the innkeeper had sold us.

"The people we passed on our way seemed harmless enough," Niels said between mouthfuls. "They can't know what's going on in Oxford."

"What's happening?" Eilaf asked.

"Bloody murder. The Saxons turned on the Danes and are butchering us. I tried to rescue my sister but she fled among those who sought sanctuary in the Church of Saint Frideswide." His voice broke, "They murdered the children. I saw my niece killed. I couldn't do anything to save her. Only seven years old." Tears coursed down his cheeks and I flung myself at him to hug our new friend. We stayed like this for some minutes, then gently, he removed my arms.

"Thank you, Ulf," he said, "we must carry this grave news to King Sweyn in Denmark. He will avenge his sister as I will exact retribution for mine."

"But she may be safe in the church," Eilaf sought to console him.

The leather-worker shook his head and winced with pain. He stepped down to the brook and rinsed the blood from his scalp.

"It stings but it can be only a scratch; see it bleeds no more. The rabid curs set fire to the church. My wife-brother died trying to stop them. To no avail. It blazed like a furnace when I left. I could not *save them*." The last words turned into a hopeless wail.

Niels sat with his head in his hands, lost in the horror of his thoughts.

"Don't worry," Eilaf muttered to me, "soon we'll be home safe with our father."

We set off once more, relieved that travellers we encountered on the road hailed us with a friendly greeting or a wave. We hastened through a small village and once clear, Niels told us to seek a footpath to the left of the thoroughfare. I spotted it first and we followed it up a rise and over to where the land began to drop down to the Trent.

"We follow the river for the rest of the way," Niels said, "unless it becomes marshy."

Fortunately it hadn't rained in recent weeks, though the weather was as dull as usual at this time of year.

"Niels?" I said.

"What?"

"Why is King Aethelred killing our people?"

"The mob in Oxford accused the Danes of meaning to kill the King and his advisers, to take over the land. It must be a lie...but if Aethelred believes it..."

"What do you think, Niels?"

The burly Dane put a hand on my shoulder, "Me, Ulf? It don't matter what I think. It's what the Forkbeard thinks that matters. Our job is to tell him what we've seen, as soon as we can."

"Does the King really have a forked beard?"

"Why else would they call him that, young Ulf?"

It pleased me to see Niels smile again. He had been so sad.

"And what about King Aethelred? Does he have a name too?"

"They saddle him with the Unread."

"Unread? Why?"

"It means '*Ill-advised*' in the Saxon tongue. I think it's because he keeps on making mistakes."

"Mistakes? Like sending that man to kill us and Gunnhild?"

"That's what I mean, Ulf, and I think that will be his biggest mistake of his life."

"Will it be war?" Eilaf interrupted.

"I'm sure of it."

"I wish I could fight in a battle."

Niels laughed, "You, Ulf! Not yet, you are too young to hoist a shield. Even Eilaf will wait three years until he builds a man's muscles, isn't it so, Eilaf?"

My brother sighed and agreed, "But when I'm older I'll come back to slay the Saxons."

"I'm afraid I can't delay that long. I hope King Sweyn will be ready and willing to move at once, but with winter in the air..."

His eyes took on a far-away semblance and he said no more.

We came to the top of a knoll. From there, the wide River Trent snaked below into the distance.

"Not far now, lads," Niels crowed, stretching to point to the horizon, "if your eyes are keen, you'll see a small building yonder and next to it a mast. It ought to be our Stefan's ship."

"Where?" I squinted without success.

"There!" Eilaf squawked with delight. "Use my finger as a sighter."

I discerned the grey shape of a tall, straight line and a small square next to it.

"I see it!"

"When we get there, we'll be safe...until we sail into the open sea, at any rate," Niels said.

I felt the energy surge into my weary legs – we were drawing near.

"Niels, it would be easy to mistake one of you for the other!" Eilaf cried, gazing at Stefan.

My brother spoke truly; the man bore a remarkable resemblance to Niels, being no more than two inches taller but with the same blue eyes and identical laughter wrinkles.

"We are sons of brothers," Niels explained before leading his cousin some yards away from us where a low, intense exchange took place.

We could not catch their words until Stefan raised his voice, "It's impossible. How am I supposed to get the crew together? We can't move."

"There's no time to waste, I tell you."

The argument proceeded until Niels stomped back to us.

"We are welcome to stay with Stefan but there is no crew to sail us to Denmark."

Happy to be in a place where we could eat and sleep, I felt safe with Niels. It didn't trouble me that we lingered in a land where Danes were regarded with hatred. Luckily, I was too young to under-stand danger that did not appear before my eyes.

"Make yourselves useful and collect wood, boil up a cauldron of water. Eel soup for lunch. I've set traps. Do you like eel?" Stefan issued commands and beamed at me.

I nodded and smiled.

"Ulf's coming with me." He disappeared into the house and came out with a wicker trug that he thrust into my hand. "Come on!"

I followed the tall trader across the meadow to the edge of a small pond. I scanned the water for eyes just above the surface. I usually steer clear of ponds to avoid the Nykken, the dark monster who shifts shape to lure children into the depths to drown them.

"Here we are," he announced, "pull on that cord, my lad."

Satisfied the pond was Nykken-free, I heaved a dripping eel trap, made of woven willow, shaped like a long sock, out of the water. Inside the snare I made out a writhing black shape.

"We've got one, Stefan!" I called.

"Bring it over here."

In a moment he had the trap open and the wriggling eel slithered on the grass, but Stefan the expert lopped off the head of the creature only for it to continue its contortions.

"Why isn't it dead?" I asked, never having seen an eel beheaded.

"Oh, it's dead, all right, eels are like that," he said trapping it under his boot. "Here," he laid the slimy creature in the trug and coiled it around on itself for a better fit. "We'll head back. Keep an eye open for goutweed or nettles."

I found some goutweed growing in the shade but Stefan shook his head.

"No good," he said, "the leaves are too old. We need young, tender ones else they're too bitter and they upset the belly. It's too late in the year, I suppose."

This is how I discovered one of Stefan's many talents: a good cook, navigator, trader and friend. He found nettles and sorted the fresh leaves he needed to add to the contents of my basket.

On our way back we came across a commotion, and this affair will explain how racial tensions were running high. We scrambled over a ditch and reached the lane that wound past a house down to the river. Drawing near to the building, voices raised in a heated argument warned of trouble. Stefan swore and his hand moved fleetingly to his sword as if to check it was still hanging by his side.

"That's Torvald they're manhandling." I narrowed my eyes to see better in the dull light, half-hoping Stefan was wrong. He was not. The shaggy-haired Torvald, one of the few members of our depleted crew, was trying to pull away from two men who, like clams, were clamped on to his arms. Three or four other men were gesticulating and shouting and it took our arrival for silence to reign.

They greeted us with hostile glares and suspicious glances into my basket. This was the first time I experienced collective hostility aimed at my person and because I belonged to a different nation.

They were wrong about me, in their ignorance, for I am no Dane, but the danger was still the same.

"More thieving Danes!" one cried.

"There are no thieves here," Torvald cried, receiving a back-handed slap across the mouth that left his lip bleeding.

"We caught this man raiding our hen coop and–"

"It's a lie!" Torvald shouted and writhed to break free, in vain.

"Where are the eggs he's taken?" Stefan asked with good reason.

"He must have put them back when we raised the hue and cry. If he's not a thief, why was he lurking by the coop?"

Stefan stared at our companion, raised an eyebrow and uttered one word, "Well?"

"I told them," his speech was indistinct as he spat blood from his split lip, "I saw a fox creeping behind the hen house and I wanted to scare it off. Doing them a favour, I was. I hoped to buy some eggs."

"That's what the mealy-mouthed scoundrel told us. But when we searched him, we found he had no coin to buy with." The taller of the two men restraining Torvald snorted the last words.

"What do you mean to do with our comrade?" Stefan asked.

"What we always do with thieves – cut off his hand," the same man said.

"But he has stolen nothing. What justice is that?"

"The land is overrun by you filthy, robbing Danes."

Stefan's hand flew to his sword and I feared the worse. But his words belied his gesture.

"Be not so hasty, Saxon. A man does not lose his hand for an unproved accusation. That is not justice. A wiser decision must be made if we are to avoid bloodshed on a greater scale."

An older man with traces of grey in his hair spoke for the first time.

"It's custom in these cases, hereabouts, to let God decide a man's guilt or innocence. Let us hie to the church and the priest will decide. What say you, Dane? It's either that or we lop off his hand here and now."

"We do not share belief in your God but your words are fair enough, Saxon. We will accompany you."

I trailed along next to Stefan and whispered, "How will their God decide, Stefan?"

Used to his constant good cheer, his black look and tense snarl dismayed me.

"Hush your questions, Ulf. Now is not the time."

The priest was a sallow-faced fellow in a soiled green tunic. After listening to the accusation, denials and Stefan's protestations, and the aggressive demands for the removal of the 'thief's' hand, he showed he did not have the strength of character to dismiss the matter.

"We must let God in His wisdom and mercy decide," he said to satisfied growls.

We trudged to a remote part of the church where they emptied pails of water, drawn from a well in the churchyard, into a cauldron.

"Hold!" cried the cleric, "the crime is not so grave that we should go beyond the elbow." To test its depth, he plunged his arm into the water. His eye for a measure was perfect and he displayed his sleeve sodden to the hollow of his forearm. Next, he found a smooth round stone, the size of a plum, and placed it on the bottom of the iron pot. They lit a fire under the huge container and everyone but two accusers, Stefan, I and the priest had to leave the building. The clergyman invited us to ascertain the water boiled. He then sprinkled the five of us with what he called holy water. Luckily, it was cold. We had to kiss a cross and a book for some reason and he told us not to speak but to pray to God to reveal the truth.

The weird trial continued with this churchman singing in a strange language in his croaking voice. When he had finished, he signalled Torvald to plunge his hand into the boiling water and draw out the stone. I gazed on, horrified, as our comrade did as bidden without any sign of sufferance except a tightening of his jaw. The priest immediately bound up his arm in a clean cloth and sealed it with a seal of the church made of molten wax.

"We will hold him for three days under guard. If after that time, the seal is unbroken and the arm is clean, he is innocent of the charge. If there is a foul, festering wound, he is guilty."

I ground my teeth in rage. What chance had a man of not blistering from such a scald? But Stefan shook my shoulder and whispered to me to hold my tongue. I obeyed, but well away from the church I pestered my friend on the way to the river.

"Stefan, why did you not slay the priest and the two Saxons in the church when you had the chance? We could have rescued Torvald from that torture."

"Would you have done that, young Ulf?"

"Ay. I would," I said with the unconsidered fire of youth.

"As a consequence, we would have had every Saxon in the shire after our blood. Did you think of that, Ulf?"

Feeling foolish, I flushed and walked on in silence.

At the house, he gutted and flayed the eel before chopping it into pieces, which he threw into the bubbling water, and added mace, wild onions and horseradish. Occasionally, he glanced at me to see whether I was sulking. But Stefan had taken a liking to me, so he handed me four crab apples.

"Peel these, core and quarter them and toss them in the pot."

We all agreed the stew was delicious and when Eilaf made to thank him, Stefan chuckled and said, "Better praise your brother: Ulf caught the eel and prepared the apples," he winked at me and his grin grew wider. It was impossible to hold a grudge against such a fellow.

I thought all was well until I settled down by the hearth that night, where I could not find sleep. Nightmarish visions of the gaping gash across Gunnhild's throat tormented me. This was nothing new but the horrible festered arm of Torvald was, so I tossed and turned, groaned and sighed until I felt an arm raise my shoulders. Stefan brought a leather flask to my lips.

"Hush, drink this."

A fiery liquid burnt my stomach.

"Sleep!"

Whatever the drink Stefan had given me, it worked like magic. When I woke in the morning, grateful and glad for a refreshing night's rest, all three teased me for being a sleepyhead. My mouth tasted sour but after some draughts of fresh water I was fit to face the day.

A commotion before midday brought Eilaf and me outdoors from our dice game to gape at a group of men, who were surrounding Stefan and raising their voices.

"We must get away!" One of the men grasped Stefan's arm who shrugged him off.

"Are you sure nobody followed you?"

"No, I told you! They burnt the church with the people inside. Oh, the screams! The evil bastards!"

For a moment, I thought he meant the church of the day before, down the lane. It took a moment to realise he meant the church in Oxford.

Niels blanched and swayed on his feet. Stefan steadied him and whispered something in his ear.

"Did you see that with your own eyes?" Niels stared imploringly at the man who had spoken.

"I'm sorry. I did. No-one survived that blaze."

"The Saxon dogs! They'll pay for this, by Odin!"

"We must flee," the first man repeated, urgency in his voice. "What started in Oxford will spread throughout the land." After the story of the hen coop, I had no doubt this was true.

"I can't move the ship with less than half a crew, it's impossible."

"We can make for the Danelaw," another red-haired man added.

"Not overland, it's too dangerous," the first man said.

"You can stay here for a day or two. If we stick together we'll have more chance of surviving. Meanwhile, others of the crew might come back to the ship."

Stefan's words proved true. Already in the afternoon two groups of men arrived with more tales of violence. The second group bore the signs of conflict; among them two wounded men bound with blood-stained bandages. Others wore tunics spattered with blood. Their tales of atrocities committed against the Danes scared me. Stefan's words comforted me: "Where else will my men flee to if not to their ship? Another ten men and we cast off."

They did not come that night but neither did any marauding Saxons. In Niels's opinion, the enemy would take action in the towns and villages settled by Danes. The next group to arrive confirmed this because although only two of them were Stefan's crew members, they led seven men, four women and six children to the ship.

"The Saxons burnt our village to the ground, shouting that we Danes had sprung up like cockle amongst the wheat!" a grey-bearded bald man said. "They chanted it repeatedly. Everything we worked for has been devoured by flames!"

One of the women began to cry and a small girl clung to her dress while her husband comforted her.

"We're still four men short to man the oars," Stefan grumbled.

The crying woman looked up with a tear-wetted face.

"I can row as well as any man," she said, wiping her eyes with fierce determination.

"Ay, me too," another of the women said.

"I can try."

"Me too."

The other women chorused in their desperation to flee from the horror afflicting their lives.

"We can give it a go," Stefan said, to a rousing cheer, but with his voice sceptical. "Gather your belongings and step on board," he called.

I dashed indoors to retrieve our dice, slipping them into my pride and joy, my new pouch. Life was good! We were on our way. But what about Torvald? I need not have worried. Stefan pointed out the wisdom of leaving the next morn at first light to put greater distance between us and this area by nightfall. With too few hours before darkness, this day, we would still be in an area fraught with danger. But I knew he was stalling in order not to leave our comrade behind.

The next morning, Stefan woke me and told me to dress in haste. In no time, we approached the church. One man with a spear stood on guard in front of a small hut close to the church. Later, I learnt that the gravediggers' tools were stored there. Torvald had spent three days nursing his arm, I supposed. Then the strangest thing happened. The priest came to unlock the hut and to shake Torvald into wake-fulness.

"We must unbind you outside by the light of day, Dane." He then began to mutter a prayer in his strange language before checking and then breaking the wax seal. Satisfied no-one had tampered with the binding, gently he unwound the bandage and where I expected to see angry red flesh covered in blisters, I saw only the tanned, hairy arm of Torvald, apparently unharmed.

"There, what did I tell you?" Torvald cried, "I stole nought and am no thief".

The Saxons hurrying to the churchyard gathered round and insisted on examining his arm, poking and prodding, but nothing would change their God's decision.

Down the lane, I turned to our comrade.

"Oi, Torvald," I said, "do you believe their God proved you innocent?"

He chortled and shook his head. "There's a trick, young 'un. You see, you have to concentrate and persuade your body it's cold water you're plunging into. Dead easy!"

I gasped in amazement and thought that easier to say than to do. Some yards farther down the lane, I asked, "Did you really see a fox, Torvald?"

The shaggy-haired villain bellowed with laughter, "Don't be daft, lad!"

As soon as we got back to the ship, Torvald told his tale to general wonderment. It heartened everyone for the journey ahead as they shared in merriment at the expense of the Saxon oppressors. The crew rowed us into the wider river, past the bustling port of London and down to the estuary. None of the ships we passed posed any danger and the women pulled on their oars without stopping or complaining. I'm sure they were relieved when Stefan steered us to a mooring place. He did not want to go out into the North Sea at night.

That pleased me, for how many times had I sat wide-eyed at tales of Draugen in my father's hall? The monster, covered in seaweed, erupts in a hideous scream when he appears and whips up terrible storms at sea at night, drowning sailors and fishermen and sinking their ships.

We would sail in the morning and Draugen couldn't harm us then since he'd be asleep on his weed-strewn seabed. Soon, I'd be safe at home with my family.

3

HEIDABY, DENMARK 1002 AD

It was later in life when I had my own long-ship that I became aware only a fool would venture across the North Sea in November. At nine, I had no inkling of normal: the captain should wait for a fair breeze blowing from the south-west and for clear skies and settled weather. At times, for others less fortunate, the delay might seem interminable, but we enjoyed good luck and the prevailing wind from that quarter. So, we set off early next morning immediately after Stefan sacrificed a squealing, wriggling piglet to the gods, its blood meant to favour our safe crossing.

The sea is bounteous and provides for man but is also capricious and perilous. Stefan shared much of his lore with me, not with Eilaf; I suppose my natural curiosity gratified him. He explained how to use the sun shadow stick – a flat wooden disk with a pointer sticking up in its centre. He floated the disk in a pail of seawater, so it kept horizontal in spite of the pitching ship. The pointer cast a shadow on the disk. With the sun right overhead, at midday, the shadow, at its shortest, pointed due north. At this time of year the shadow was weak, but when I squeaked that we were heading north-east, he ruffled my hair and looked pleased.

In the afternoon, Stefan indicated away to the east. "Seabirds," he said, "what does that mean, Ulf?"

I thought for a second and replied, "Land, Stefan?"

"Right, probably an island," he said, but I believe he knew exactly which one.

The journey proved interesting but not much fun. The spray soaked us as we pitched and rolled. Some of the children were sick and chilled by the wind. There was no question of lighting a fire in our wooden ship, so cold salt meat and bread were offered. In any case, the bottom of our boat was awash with seawater and Eilaf and I, our feet wet and numb, helped the men bail out.

After hours of sailing, Eilaf asked Niels why the men were taking down our dragon figurehead.

"See yon grey line over there? Ay? It's the coast of Denmark and we must not anger or frighten the spirits of the land or they will turn against us."

"So we are almost there?"

"Soon we'll sight the estuary of the River Eider where we'll take down the sail."

"So it's back to rowing again. Can Ulf and I take an oar, please, Niels, please!"

"I'll have to ask Stefan," he said, stepping astern where our captain was talking to the helmsman.

Stefan looked our way, turned back to Niels with a shake of his head and Niels gesticulated towards us. Our impatient wait ended with these words:

"Stefan says if you don't keep rhythm with the others and your oar flies out of the water, you're straight off the rowing."

"We'll do it right, won't we, Ulf!"

And we did. Heavy work for two young boys, but we kept up with the men and women near us. I felt very grown-up and impor-tant. Too busy concentrating on my task at the time, I don't remember the sights, but we must have steered from the Eider estuary into the River Treene. Stefan barked out orders and we slowed our rowing. By now, Eilaf and I were red-faced and the earlier numbness became but a distant memory. Like the others on our side of the ship, we heaved in the heavy oars as the craft glided next to a jetty.

"Home!" Niels shouted and we all cheered and bowed our heads to say a prayer for our safe arrival.

"We make camp near the village," Stefan announced. "and march to Heidaby in the morning."

"Is it far?" I asked Niels as he tied up the stern of our ship to the dock.

"About three leagues, Ulf. We'll be there before midday and maybe you'll meet King Sweyn."

"Is he in Heidaby?"

"If he isn't, you won't meet him, will you?"

I decided to leave Niels to get on with his tasks. My father, at home in Sweden, hated being pestered when he had work to do. At this thought, I felt a strange mixture of sadness and relief. The latter because we were safe among friends, but who knew how long it would be before I embraced my parents once more? I hadn't seen them or our sister Gytha for two years; she would be seven winters old by now, but I would still be taller than her, I hoped.

In the evening, the friendly people of the village brought us a large cauldron of bubbling fish soup. The delicious meal, together with our campfires, warmed our cold bodies. The men drank and sang songs but the cheer was strained. Many of them lapsed into gloomy silences and stared into the flames – a fiery reminder of recent horrors. I knew their thoughts were far away in Oxford and on what had happened there. I overheard some men talking about revenge. They all agreed about the problem of crossing the sea again in this season. There could be no swift retribution. This was when I first realised how lucky we had been with the weather. Lucky? Or favoured by the gods? I knew not which. From listening, I realised how uncommon it was to cross the North Sea in November.

I made friends with a boy named Lars, who taught me how to play a game he called 'split the kipper'. It consisted of standing face to face with each other, feet together, a yard apart, and taking it in turns to throw his knife near the foot of the other. Then he had to stretch to place it next to the blade. The first to make the other fail to reach as far as the marker lost the game.

Lars won and I looked at his knife with longing.

"Do you want it?" he asked. "You can't have it. Unless you want to swap for that."

"I can't give you my pouch. It is a gift. But I can give you this."

I held out my silver coin. Lars snatched it from me and relinquished the knife. We grinned at each other at the done deal. Now I had a knife like Eilaf, but mine had a whalebone hilt and I thought it much superior.

Niels proved right, of course, and next day we strode into Heidaby before midday. It confused me to find the capital of Denmark a port. So why hadn't we sailed into it?

"Better to hike three leagues, Ulf, than to take the dangerous voyage far to the north to sail around the peninsula of Denmark." Stefan asked for my knife and I handed it over feeling manly and proud. He used it to sketch a map of Denmark in the earth; it was so clear I understood what he meant at once. We had sailed into the neck of the land by estuary and river and crossed the remaining part to reach the opposite coast.

"This is the North Sea. This is the Baltic."

I ran down the straight street that lay parallel to others, all lined with tightly packed houses, each leading to a jetty, for my first glimpse of the Danish Baltic. Another time, I would ask Stefan in which direction Sweden lay. I knew my homeland had a Baltic coast, I had heard father say so.

In Heidaby, the people's custom of painting around their eyes struck me as odd. They all did it; men and women used different colours but most of the men preferred blue patterns. It made them look fierce, especially those that ended in points down their cheeks as far as their shaggy beards.

Stefan and Niels disappeared into the King's Hall, leaving us boys to our own devices. We explored the port and admired the different ships while soaking up the different smells of fish and tar. I loved the pungent odour of molten tar and even today, a whiff of it takes me straight back to my boyhood in Heidaby. The cries and greetings of the sailors and fishermen gave a magical atmosphere to my surroundings. Many trading vessels, shorter and broader than Stefan's long-ship, were centres of activity. I watched one such *knarr* being loaded with cups, tableware, glass beads, and pottery. Other objects included bone and antler combs, leather goods, jewellery, and cloth. Not to mention the blacksmiths and armour makers' products that appealed to me: swords, battle axes, chainmail and body armour. Another ship unloaded things I'd never seen before: fabrics, spices, silk, strange fruits, large earthenware jars of wine and oil and other goods of the south. I wondered if they sailed around the Danis\h peninsula. Later, when I asked Stefan, he told me they rowed out of the Baltic down a river with an unusual name, the Dnieper. After-wards, they joined other rivers and lakes to take them to the ends of the world. I would like to go there.

"So, this is where you have disappeared to," the familiar voice of Niels greeted us.

"Niels!"

"Come on, I've got a surprise for you!"

We followed his long strides at a run, breathlessly exchanging ideas about what might await us. If Niels heard us, he ignored our chatter. Neither of us could have imagined the thrill to come in the King's Hall.

The imposing construction stood in the middle of the settlement. A series of beams planted into the ground leant at an angle to support the front wall of the reed-thatched building, its eaves overhanging almost down to my height. Squawking gulls flapped off the roof at our hurried arrival. Niels led us to the second door at the far end of the hall. The gloomy interior, lit only by a small window in the back wall, made it hard for my eyes to adjust. Eilaf discerned what was going on more clearly.

"Father!" he cried.

The outline of a tall, fur-clad man bent to receive Eilaf's outflung arms in an embrace. Jealousy and joy drove me to pile in on them. "Steady on, Ulf," my father's stern voice reproved me. He had to stretch a hand to the ground to stop himself toppling over from his squatting position.

"Why are you in Heidaby?" I gasped.

"I would ask you both the same question if I didn't know the answer," father said, his voice dark with menace. "Come, boys, others await you."

This time, I beat Eilaf to mother. I spied her gazing at us from the shadows near a wall. Lovelier than I envisioned her in fanciful imagination in our English exile. Her long blonde hair cascaded from under a knotted kerchief over her shoulders on a deep blue, ankle-length over-dress with multi-coloured trimmings at the cuffs and down the opening. A lovely tri-lobed brooch held it closed. Under this outer garment, she wore a pale blue woollen dress and I could see other clasps closing its straps. All these details were obscured by the warmth of her smile as she gathered me to her bosom. I thought my heart might burst with happiness.

"Did they ill-use you in England?" she whispered.

"Not me," I said, "Ma, I rowed Stefan's ship and I have a knife of my own!"

She laughed but her eyes were full of tears of joy as she pushed me away.

"Let me greet your brother."

I discovered later that father had come to Heidaby at the request of King Sweyn. He wanted to enlist father's support in the case of a Norwegian assault to retake lands ceded, after defeat to the joint Swedish-Danish victory. Father explained how Sweyn had never forgotten his failed attempt to take London in 998 and proposed to try again. However, the tragic events in England had changed his plans. No longer did he plan a raid for plunder but for something more severe. He wished to punish Aethelred for the death of his sister and brother-in-law and for what he had done to our folk in Oxford.

We wintered in Heidaby and I became firm friends with King Sweyn's second son, Cnut, who was a year older than me, and with his younger sister Estrid. We got up to all the usual pranks youngsters perpetrate at that age but I now realise that my feelings for Estrid were not just those of friendship. Later we would marry and have children, but I must not get too far ahead of myself. Suffice it to say, this year transformed from the most traumatic into the happiest of my childhood.

I grew impatient to become a warrior. Wrestling with Cnut and Eilaf was of little account for I grew up with legends of my great-grandfather being a white bear. According to the lore, it sired my grandfather Bjørn with a Swedish noblewoman. I flattered myself that I grew as strong as a bear cub and explained away my defeats to Eilaf by him having the same inherited strength. My father's nick-name was *'Fleetfoot'*, so it was no surprise I excelled at racing. I was faster than Eilaf, but these things mattered not while I fretted to grow into manhood.

Our home in Upsal awaited us in the spring but we returned without father, Stefan and Niels, who agreed to take part in Sweyn Forkbeard's attack on England. King Sweyn ordered a jarl, Asbeorn, to accompany us home and to protect us there in the event of Norwegian or brigand raids. In Heidaby I heard whisperings that Asbeorn was Sweyn's son, but the King did not recognise his paternity. For sure, Sweyn's wife, Gunhild, snubbed the jarl and seemed pleased at his mission away in Upsal. I liked Asbeorn; there was a nobility about him suggesting the tales were true, and he agreed to teach me how to wield a sword. We practised with wooden swords for hours on end. Best of all, he refused to practise with Eilaf on the grounds that I'd asked first. It made wrestling with my brother something to avoid because he behaved resentfully and vindictively.

Another two years passed before I saw father again but when he returned, he came as a conquering hero laden with bounty. In front of a roaring fire on winter's evenings, he regaled us with tales of what happened on campaign. Typical of those years, their adventure began with a betrayal. Although committed in their favour, father's stern features hardened when he told us the French reeve of Queen Emma betrayed the town of Exeter so the host seized much treasure.

We boys wanted to hear about these victories and not be subjected to a long diatribe about treachery. Father impressed upon our young minds at length the importance of uprightness that remained with us in our adult lives. After Exeter, the Danish force swept on inland to Wilton, which it ravaged and burnt. Thence, it moved to attack Salisbury before returning to the sea. King Sweyn decided that Aethelred and the Saxons had not been punished enough and that there remained more wealth to plunder. The Isle of Wight offered winter quarters for the ships.

With the new year of 1004, the host sailed to East Anglia where they ravaged and burnt the burh of Norwich. Here, father paused to praise an enemy and instilled in us respect for a worthy foe. "A certain Ulfcytel, with the witan of East Anglia, decided it better to purchase peace from our force before we did enormous damage through the land. We had come upon the Angles unawares and Ulfcytel had not time to gather his army."

"Buy peace!" Eilaf exclaimed, "This Ulfcytel is a coward then!"

Eilaf expressed my thoughts but luckily I did not say anything. Father's iron hand rattled every tooth in Eilaf's head, leaving an angry red mark across his face and tears in his eyes.

" I pray Odin you become half the man Ulfcytel is, boy!" father hissed at Eilaf. "Sweyn did a treacherous thing. Three weeks later, under cover of the truce he should have kept between them, he stole inland from the ships and marched on Thetford."

"That was wrong of King Sweyn," I said, earning a look of approval from father and a glare from Eilaf.

"We burnt and ravaged Thetford. In the morning, about to return to our ships, Ulfcytel came with his force to fight us and fought so fiercely he created huge loss of life on both sides. The noblest men of

East Anglia fell that day on the battlefield, otherwise we would not have made it to our ships and I would not be telling this tale today. I have never met harder hand to hand fighting in England than Ulfcytel brought against us."

"Sorry, father," Eilaf muttered and gained himself a hair-ruffling from Thorgils Fleetfoot.

"Lucky for us King Sweyn ordered fortification of the beach-head and left a substantial guard on our ships, else all would have been lost. Ulfcytel sent a force to hew the ships apart but our men repulsed it and we made our escape. In any case, a great famine swept over England, so King Sweyn decided to return and here I am. I do not believe the Forkbeard is satisfied. He will sail back to England."

"If he does, father, may I come too?" Eilaf asked.

A long pause followed as father stared into the dancing flames in the hearth. I held my breath because if he took Eilaf with him, I might plead to go along with them.

"I don't see why not," he said at last. "After all, King Sweyn took Cnut with him."

"But Cnut is my age," I protested, "take me, father, please."

"Cnut is a year older than you," Eilaf said dismissively.

"Thorgils, do you think it wise?" Mother looked stricken. "The boys are too young."

"And you would keep them clinging to your skirts when they have grey beards, Sigrid."

"My mind is made up, Eilaf will come with me. Ulf will stay to protect you and Gytha."

"I'd be safer protecting myself," Gytha murmured too low for father to hear, but I did.

She'd be safer with me and my consolidated sword skills than she would be with Eilaf, for sure. But this thought was of little consolation until father gazed at my crestfallen countenance, "Cheer up Ulf, you have my word I'll take you on the next-but-one campaign."

4

UPSAL, SPRING 1006 AD

The spring equinox came three weeks after father and Eilaf
departed for England. Eilaf, overjoyed, might have spared his
torments like: 'Shall I greet Niels and Stefan for you, Ulf?' – and
many more provocations. Once father's ship slipped out of the
harbour, mother insisted we joined with others in the traditional visit
to the temple at Upsal to make a sacrifice to Odin. This rite served to
invoke strength and fortune for our men gone to war.

The construction, in a hollow surrounded by hills, stood by a
sacred grove with a spring, so was easily sighted as we approached.
Around the temple, a golden chain hung from the gables. Nine males
of different species were to be sacrificed – we led a goat – other families brought an Irish slave, a horse, ram, dog, donkey, gander, cockerel,
bullock and hog.

The grove frightened me when I was little. Of course, I had been
away for two years so my memory was of childhood fears. I must have
been five when I had last gazed upon the dogs and horses hanging
among the rotting corpses of men. The building, richly carved and
adorned with gold, contained the images of three of our gods sitting
on a triple throne: on the central one sat the mighty Thor, holding a

mace, and on either side, Odin and Freyr. Odin wore armour, Freyr, instead, sat there with an immense erect penis.

We sought out the priest of Odin to conduct the ceremonial sacrifice on behalf of our warriors. Blood placates the gods but, the priest told us, the human offering would be different. The slave would be bound hand and foot and thrown into the depths of the spring where he ought not to resurface for the sacrifice to be acceptable to the gods. We stared at the crystalline waters, anxious that the red-haired man would not reappear but we saw only a decreasing number of bubbles break the surface. It seemed the gods, pleased by the offering, decreed he would not surface. A rousing cheer broke from our group. The diviner expressed satisfaction and the folk began to sing.

One by one, the priest slit the throats of the animals, spilling their blood on the ground. To avoid trouble, while they were placid, the hog and the dog, being the more intelligent of the beasts according to the wizen-faced official, met their doom first. The ceremony lasted too long for my taste and the blood and corpses disgusted me, although I knew the sacrifices would help to protect my family at war and strengthen their sinews. I confess my relief on leaving the grove.

Mother teased me as we left the sacred place behind, "Ulf, you look so pale, anyone'd think *you'd* had your blood drained!"

"I'm all right!"

We returned home, whereas others had to wait up to nine days for their sacrificial ceremonies. The thought of spending so long, including nights, at the temple, made me shudder. My reaction made me doubt myself: if the place unmanned me, what use would I be in battle?

The only person I could share my worries with was Asbeorn. He chose not to return to Denmark, claiming that he preferred Upsal to Heidaby. His untruths did not deceive us. We all knew he had lost his heart to my cousin, Lykke. They spent so much time gazing into each other's eyes, she blushing and he grinning, only a blind man might not know they were smitten. I had my own selfish reasons to be overjoyed that Asbeorn was staying with us. Apart from training me in battle-craft, he had become my only confidant. I confessed to him my experience at the grove.

"It's normal, Ulf. I don't like sacrifices either. It's not as if the victims can fight back, is it? If it repulses me, it doesn't signify I'm feeble, does it?"

He grinned and flexed an arm to show off his bulging muscles.

"It's as well I didn't sail with father. I'd have let him down."

"As well for the Saxons, you mean? Eilaf's gone and he's less than half the warrior you are."

"Are you serious, Asbeorn? Swear it!"

"Nothing more I can teach you. Not alone, at any rate."

"What is your meaning?"

"Look, Ulf, in battle it's likely you will be attacked by more than one enemy at a time and you need to know how to resist and overcome them."

"How can I learn that?"

"Leave it to me," he said, "and stop worrying about being man enough. You'll make a name for yourself as a hero, all in good time."

He left me to think about this. The next day I learnt how to manage a shield and a battle-axe against an imaginary additional foe. It irritated me to make moves against a pretend opponent, but Asbeorn convinced me it was better this way and once more he proved to be right. Some days of this paid off after he enlisted two of the local youths to join our training. They were willing sparring partners and strapping fellows only too pleased to vaunt their burly muscles. Every healthy young Swede loves a fight. The difference in the routine left me bruised, breathless and eager for more. My reflexes sharpened and the harder the odds against me, the more confident and trusting I grew in my skills.

"You are almost ready Ulf," Asbeorn told me, "one more lesson to learn."

"What's – ow! What was that for?"

I glared, my ear red and ringing from the unexpected blow the Dane delivered.

"Never be taken by surprise."

"Ow!"

I didn't think he would do it again but he did and I leapt at him for vengeance but he was ready and I landed flat on my back, the wind knocked out of me. I curled up in a vain attempt to protect myself as he kicked me repeatedly.

"Stop that, you beast!" Lykke intervened, appearing from behind a pile of hay from whence she'd been spying on us, dragging at his arm, "What do you think you're doing? That's my cousin you're laying into!"

"I'm training him."

"To be a cripple?"

"Lykke, this is men's stuff. Why don't you mind your own business?"

Asbeorn caught her wrist to save his own ear but, distracted, he didn't see me rise to take up a practice sword...the first he knew was a stinging fire across the buttocks.

"Aaargh!" He released Lykke and spun round in time to dodge another fierce blow from the wooden sword.

"Well done, Ulf, crack him another!"

Asbeorn glared at Lykke and grinned at me.

"You learn fast, Ulf. It's important to catch your enemy when he least expects it. Ow!"

Smirking, Lykke landed him a mighty cuff across the head.

"For kicking my cousin when on the ground."

"Lykke!" he called after her but she ignored him and marched straight-backed, blonde plait swinging, into our hall.

"Go after her, Asbeorn. It's all right. Anyhow, I've suffered enough for today." I ached all over but had learnt a valuable lesson. I vowed to myself, as Asbeorn followed my advice, that nobody would take Ulf Thorgilsson unawares ever again. I noticed, with a wry smile, how he glanced back twice to check on my sincerity.

Five months passed from the time of father's departure when a trading knarr tied up in the harbour. One of the men who departed with him, a tall warrior with piercing blue eyes named Brede, strolled into our hall. I did not notice at once, as he greeted mother with the news that her menfolk were well, but as he turned to acknowledge me I could not hide my dismay.

"Master Ulf, you see I left some of me behind in England with the bloody Saxons!"

His right arm ended in a stump below the elbow. "I'm no use now. I'm back to catch fish and to annoy my Helga. I'll have Knud fashion me a hook and a harness for it in his forge. Then I'll be able to carry baskets and such like."

"I'm sorry, Brede. Was the fighting terrible?"

"It always is, Ulf. You can't afford a moment's distraction in the shield-wall. A Saxon axe did for me. We landed at Sandwich and took the town. From there we raided through the whole country and gathered much wealth. I brought you this."

I'd been wondering what he was keeping hidden under his cloak, clutched so tightly to his chest. He fumbled to prevent it from falling to the floor and swore under his breath. "Here! Lend a hand," he said, laughing bitterly at the intentional irony.

A sword in a tooled leather sheath, its walrus tusk hilt bound with a spiral of gold wire!

"Take it, Ulf, it's yours."

I gasped in wonderment, "Thank you, Brede, is it really for me?"

"Don't thank me, Ulf. This is a gift from your father. He took it from a Saxon thegn he slew in a ferocious fight. Eilaf wanted it, but Thorgils said he would have to slay his own Saxon to win a sword." Brede's laugh came harsh and grating. I had the feeling he did not like my brother.

"But I didn't kill anyone to deserve the sword. Why did father send it to me?"

"He watched you practising with the Dane before he left. I remember him boasting that you will be a mighty warrior like him."

I swelled with pride but did not let it show; my bruises were too fresh and my ear still fiery-red from my lesson. I drew the sword and

35

swept it through the air like an experienced warrior. Oh, why did the years also not sweep past so I could fight the Saxons?

I sat drinking ale with Brede, who finished his account of the campaign up to when he left the host.

"While we were raiding in Kent, the Saxons from Wessex joined with the Angles from Mercia and we evaded them as they outnumbered us two to one. By now, the leaves on the trees had begun to change colour – it's a sight, Ulf! Ours are mostly green all year but that Saxon foliage puts on a show...reds, yellows and gold. They shed their leaves to make a colourful carpet." He took another deep draught of ale. "Anyway, we decided to head for the ships. An enemy force tried to cut us off and that's where I lost my hand but it cost them far more men than us. King Sweyn sailed over to the large isle off the coast, called Wight. It has fine sheltered harbours so there they will stay over winter but I believe the King is planning surprise raids in that season into Hampshire. If we catch them when they least expect us they will have no time to gather their forces. Pity is, I won't be there to share in the spoils." He stared glumly at the stump of his arm and I noticed the pallor and gloominess of our guest for the first time. A man cannot recover fast from the loss of a limb.

I reflected on what he told me and came to the conclusion, not wrongly, that much of warfare is based on surprise, be it in the shield-wall or when devising tactics. Another thought occurred to me: my father would not be home for winter as I'd hoped, so I would have to wait a year and another before going on the campaign. Thirteen autumns I had lived if my calculations were correct. I would be fifteen when I went into battle. As it turned out I would be older, but I was determined to spend the next two years building my strength by lifting weights, running and practising fighting.

Life rarely goes according to plan and my proposed practice combat soon became replaced by the real thing. One morning in late autumn, two long-ships sailed towards Upsal. I hoped one was bearing father home from England although I ought to have realised, from Brede's words, how unlikely it was. When the ships drew nearer, we could see the sails boasted unknown emblems: black ravens on a light blue ground. The pale blue merged into the sky and sea, creating the strange effect of thrusting the black birds to meet the onlooker's eye.

Warning horns blared in our town and I hurried indoors to seize my sword and shield. Asbeorn sought me out, "Stick near me Ulf and you'll be all right."

His strong presence reassured me. There were also enough warriors in Upsal to combat the threat if the strangers were hostile, since father had taken only one ship's crew to join the Danes on campaign in England.

The invaders were Norsemen. We had heard tales of their incursions in the territories captured from them by Sweyn some years ago. Once again, surprise! We expected an attack to come overland hence the internal manned watchtowers. Instead, here were the Norwegians pouring onto our jetties and heading at a run into town, bristling with axes. They were slowed down by a deluge of missiles, most parried without damage by their colourful round shields. Asbeorn and I joined the men blocking the entry to town in a shield-wall for my first experience of the fear and excitement before battle.

"Keep your shield high, like this," Asbeorn said from the corner of his mouth, locking his shield to overlap mine at the edge. The man to my right grinned and nodded approval, abutting his wooden barrier to mine. This same operation repeated all the way down the line. The Norsemen started battering their weapons against their shields to intimidate us as they advanced, and began to shout insults and whoop war cries. A strange calm settled over me, easing the previous wild thumping of my heart. My concentration overcame all the mental and physical problems I supposed might compromise my performance in battle. This quiet sensation became a blessing and a helpful characteristic of my life as a warrior. For a novice, I began well. For sure, it helped my confidence to have my tutor beside me.

"Let the foe strike the first blow," he advised, "and never take your eyes off his. Show no fear."

When the blow came, delivered by axe, it arrived so powerfully I feared to lose my footing but not only did I resist the force but I snaked out a lunge with my sword that caught my assailant off-balance, and the finely-honed blade sliced across his cheek, drawing blood. So, with my first strike in anger, I wetted my sword. Enraged, the tall, muscular brute roared and swung another mighty hit at my shield. This had been crafted in linden and gifted to me by Asbeorn, who had assured me that an older tested shield was far more resistant than a new one. How I blessed him for it as the shuddering blow set my whole body jarring. Yet the wood resisted. My counter-thrust the Norwegian swatted away with his shield and, with a hideous gap-toothed grin, renewed his assault.

I heard his nearest companion scream as Asbeorn's sword sliced into his throat. Oblivious to all else around me my eyes were fixed on but one man, he who wished to end my life. Whether we were winning the day mattered little to me in my combative trance. My personal victory had been to hold steady in the shield-wall, the next to survive the heavy battering of my foe. How to change from defence to attack? I must not take any risks, but what about my lessons? I remembered Asbeorn's advice about surprise. So I lowered my sword arm furtively with the hilt next to my knee. I made sure the enemy was unaware of my move, discovering he was intent on preparing his next swing. I let it come, took the force, then shot out my sword below his defences into his thigh. A howl of pain accompanied the shock in his eyes before he tottered and fell to his knees.

"Strike now Ulf!" called Asbeorn. For some peculiar reason, I was admiring my handiwork instead of completing the task. Like a man snapping out of a dream I pushed forward and brought my sword down, but I had given the fellow time to organise his defence and he parried the blow well with his shield. Another lesson learnt. In the end, his loss of blood did for him and I took my place again in the shield-wall. There was no replacement for the dying man because the Norsemen unwisely attacked Upsal with only two ships' crews.

Glancing to either side, I saw my companion to the right harder pressed than Asbeorn so I struck at the enemy's flank behind his shield arm. My blade sliced through his leather jerkin and, his concentration broken by the realisation of a second danger, my comrade seized the advantage and inflict a mortal wound to the chest of the invader. This freed him to aid the man to his right while I diverted my attention to Asbeorn's adversary, a shaggy-haired brute wearing a mail shirt. Again, the double assault paid off and while none of my strikes broke through his expert defence, Asbeorn now got the better of him. For the first of many times, I experienced the sense of fraternal comradeship brought by fighting for one's life and relying on a comrade.

The battle was won. Although the few survivors made to run back to their ships, we showed no mercy. At the very least, our men were determined to gain the prize of two fine Norwegian long-ships. I joined in the headlong chase and learnt that an axe is a better weapon than a sword when in pursuit. Had I known this, I would have picked one up. In one day, unsurprisingly, I discovered more about myself and warfare than thirteen years of life had taught me.

Another new experience came with the victory feast. My mother, the noble Sigrid, bestowing an honour reserved to heroes, served at our table helped by Lykke. The comradeship I referred to earlier reached fever pitch in my head that evening, so to add to my new worldliness was the literal and not-so-literal intoxication caused by boasting of our deeds and drinking vast quantities of ale. I paid for it the next day with my thunderous hangover and the incessant teasing of Lykke and mother. But I appreciated she was bursting with pride for what I had achieved. My head thumped so sorely and my stomach growled so queasily that I did not join in the stripping and burial of the dead. Others claimed trophies but my friend Asbeorn did not forget me and brought me the battle-axe that so sorely tested my shield. My first trophy! There would be many more in the future.

At the end of February, the next year, to our joy, a long-ship sailed into Upsal. Father, Eilaf and their men returned. Mother greeted Eilaf like an all-conquering warrior and I tried to curb my jealousy: I was the hero of the family.

That evening great was the feasting again, but I drank far more sensible amounts of ale and listened with interest to father explaining to Brede what had occurred after he left the host the previous autumn. Brede carried his iron hook with pride – it gave him the legendary aspect of a hero in my eyes.

"We took the Saxons by surprise one morning with a fair following wind and we sailed into Hamwic before pressing deep into Hampshire. We met little resistance and soon stocked up on live-stock. From Hampshire, we pushed on into Berkshire as far as the royal burh of Reading, where we encountered our first real opposi-tion. King Sweyn – ay, Ulf, he did return safely to Heidaby – where was I? Ah, the King decided to abandon the assault on Reading and to cross the Chiltern hills to a place called Wallingford. We sacked the town and took considerable riches."

He paused to drink and Eilaf joined in the account, "The best thing we did was to strike in a wide curve along the ridgeway into the North Wiltshire Downs. The Saxons didn't expect that did they, father?"

Thorgils smiled and lifted his glass to his eldest son, "They did not, Eilaf, and do you all remember how they quailed when we halted to invite an attack at that old earthwork with the odd name, what–?"

"Cuckhamsley Knob!" Eilaf shouted, "They were too afraid to fight."

"It's true, but then we defeated the Wiltshire fyrd at Avebury where the ridgeway crosses the River Kennet. They were tough oppo-nents, eh, Eilaf? So hard, that we decided to sweep past Winchester and return to our ships. We did so much damage that the Saxons opted to sue for peace. That gave us the chance, of course, to stipulate our conditions. Thirty-six thousand pounds in silver. In exchange, we agreed to leave English waters and here we are, the richer for our expedition."

"I wish I had been there!" I cried.

This gave my detestable brother his opening.

"Look here, little brother, see what our grateful King gifted me." As if I could have missed noticing the twisted and wrought gold arm ring. He'd never stopped fiddling with it and flexing his muscles to show it to better effect throughout the meal. "Think yourself lucky you were safe at home with mother. *You'd* have been chopped to pieces by those ferocious Saxons!" He made his laugh as sarcastic and irritating as possible.

"I think not," Asbeorn's tone was sharp. "Did you not see the two Norse ships moored when you landed? Ulf fought shoulder to shoulder with me and I defy you to find a Saxon as mighty as the warrior Ulf brought down." My friend raised his glass to me and, grateful, I replicated the gesture. Without taking my eyes off Eilaf, I said, "Father, I haven't had chance to thank you for the gift of my magnificent sword. Know you, though, I put it to good use and bloodied it."

How I enjoyed the crestfallen expression on Eilaf's face and how I delighted at father's next words, "I am sure you will put it to greater service on our next campaign to England, my lad. And you'll win yourself many an arm ring." He glowered at Eilaf to express his disapproval.

How right he was but I had to wait two more long years for that to occur – my growing and strengthening time.

5

UPSAL, NEW YEAR, 1009 AD

Two years after his return home, father called a gathering of his karls and thralls to make an announcement. Eilaf denied any knowledge of what it might concern and mother, equally unforthcoming, said, "Go to the meeting and you'll find out.

Father sat in his favourite box chair, the one with battle images carved on its side panels. Placed in the centre of the raised dais, where the high table usually stood, he overlooked the gathering crowd milling around in the body of the hall.

"Eilaf, Ulf, Asbeorn!" he called, "come and sit, here!"

I arrived first of the three and chose the seat at his right hand, which earned me a glare from my elder brother. Why four years seniority in the accident of birth should make him feel more important eluded me. With hesitation and ill-grace, he sat on the other chair that father patted impatiently. Asbeorn took the remaining place to my right, which was the real reason I had chosen to sit this side of my parent: I wanted my friend next to me.

Jarl Thorgils stood and addressed his people. The expectancy of the hush told me they were as curious as Eilaf and me.

"Friends, I called you here because there is an important decision to communicate to you all. But first, I wish to apprise you of concern regarding events overseas. King Sweyn, in Denmark, has a group of informants, and what I am about to tell you he has shared with me. As you know, we returned from a successful raid in England in this Bone Marrow Sucking month, two years ago." The silence in the hall as he paused, broken by an occasional cough, sniffing or throat clearing, typical of the cold season, indicated his audience were listening with rapt attention. "The English, from these reports, have taken counter-measures," here he sneered, "in the vain hope of warding off our renewed attacks." From the back of the hall came a sarcastic laugh in response to father's disdain and one or two others joined in.

Thorgils raised a hand, "We must not underestimate them, of course. Those who were with me before know a thing or two about the valour of our adversaries. They have revived the ealdormanry of Mercia, once a proud kingdom in its own right, under a formidable leader: Eadric Streoner. This is an attempt to provide for better defence of central England under a single command. I know him as a courageous thegn and respect his prowess, so we must destroy him. Moreover, the English have not wasted time but spent it creating a new fleet of warships. King Sweyn is annoyed. In truth, he has not forgiven the ill-treatment of our settlers," Father's voice rose to an angry climax, "culminating in the massacre in Oxford some years ago. Now, he asks me to sail with him in the spring for another expedition..." here, he hesitated, for effect, "...but I refused."

A general murmur of disapproval coursed around the hall and I stared open-mouthed at my lord and father. Eilaf's face was no less shocked than mine and Asbeorn, a true Dane, swore under his breath.

"Ay, refused...but only for myself. My decision is to stay in Upsal to attend to the strengthening of our defences. Instead, as you are aware, my son Ulf, Asbeorn here, and other brave men of this town captured two Norwegian long-ships. I intend to make a gift of them to my sons." An idle gesture of his hand indicated me and Eilaf. "Each will make the short crossing to Heidaby where they will be at the service of King Sweyn." Asbeorn swore again but this time out loud and in a positive way.

Father heard him and smiled. Aware of his esteem for Asbeorn, I still did not expect what followed. "And to you, Asbeorn, I concede my own ship and its crew. You also will travel with my sons on this expedition. Do you agree?"

Asbeorn leapt to his feet and knelt before father.

"Thank you, Lord, for the honour you bestow on your servant."

So, amid the general rowdiness of the hall, it was settled. The men, ever eager to set off for plunder and adventure, could not contain their excitement. Some hugged their friends, others argued over their priorities, while it took father a matter of moments to restore order by shouting over the commotion.

"Those wishing to sail to Denmark and thence England, other than my own crew, will have to seek their place with my sons. There will be work to do. Among other things, careening and repainting the Norse ships. The moot is over."

My father turned to me, "Do not take all comers, select the men with strength and experience of combat." He spoke so low that neither Asbeorn nor Eilaf heard. I thanked him but as I turned away, I saw my brother staring at us intently. Thus came my first inkling that the expedition would not be as straightforward as it might at first seem.

I stepped down into the hall where the press and clamour of men made my head spin. They all seemed to be trying to out-bellow each other to gain my attention. I raised a hand for silence.

"Those who wish to speak with me about the expedition must come to me at the *Sjøhingst*." Thus, I had chosen which of the two ships would be mine without consulting Eilaf. *Sjøhingst* in the Norse language means 'Sea Stallion' and the name pleased me. I can think of no other reason why I behaved so wrongly. Eilaf was soon to be more exasperated by the situation, and not just because of my roughshod avoidance of discussion. Whereas I was overwhelmed by requests for places, he was reduced to five opportunists. In short, I got to pick the best warriors, an experienced steersman and a sail-maker with the full crew complement. Incensed, he scuttled away to moan about me to father, whose reply further infuriated him. Asbeorn caught the exchange and referred back how Thorgils had explained I cut a more manly figure as a warrior and as a consequence, as a leader of men. Asbeorn also warned me, presciently as it turned out, to beware my brother's festering resentment.

Eilaf lured away my steersman by offering silver acquired in England. When I confronted him with this underhandedness, he launched himself at me, fists flying.

"Am I supposed to let you, the runt of the litter, get the upper hand?" he hissed.

"I'll show you who's the runt!"

Trained in combat over time, I was light on my feet where he was lumbering. My reflexes were honed to a sharpness he could only dream about, and this might have made for his humiliation. But it was not what I wanted. I reasoned our expedition would fail if its leaders loathed each other. I refrained from hurting him and, instead, frustrated his blows by dodging them, in the end catching his wrist, spinning him around and pinning him so I could speak in his ear.

"Brother, I did not mean to offend you and have no intention ever to harm you. Keep the steersman. I will learn that trade too."

With hindsight, I should not have added that final comment because it contained an implicit criticism of his fighting abilities and I sorely underestimated his resentful nature.

"The steersman has chosen to come with me, as will others, you'll see" he hissed, shaking off my grip. "You'd better be careful not to cross me again, little brother, for differently from you, I cannot promise not to harm you." His voice, laden with menace, made the hairs on my forearm stand like heckles and I clenched my fists ready to wipe the hatred from his face. At that moment, mother came out carrying a basket. She grinned at us both, "Having a discussion are you?"

"Not at all, mother," Eilaf smiled at her, sweetness and charm, the aggression replaced with childlike innocence, "we were just arranging our ships' crews. Ulf has been kind enough to offer me an experienced steersman, is all."

I gaped at his effrontery but took the chance to calm the turbulent waters by nodding my agreement and forcing a smile.

"That's kind of you Ulf," she said, but the shrewdness in her eyes told me we had not convinced the woman who knew us better than any other person.

I walked away, dwelling on Eilaf's words. Did he mean to entice more of my crew? Did he have sufficient money? Could all the men be bought or would some remain loyal? In reality, he had no need to pay. The rumours of his largesse attracted men enough, who would follow a generous leader on a plundering raid to the ends of the earth if required. The next month was spent in preparations. These, above all, meant me taking the *Sjøhingst* out of the harbour to familiarise myself with the steer-board and to train my crew at the simple tasks of oarsmanship and sail-raising. We need not set out for Denmark until the earliest days of spring because only then did King Sweyn expect us.

I decided to speak with the sail-maker. I expect my decision to remove the black raven was to a great extent influenced by my quarrel with Eilaf. He was no longer speaking to me, and instead ignoring my greetings and repulsing my reasoned arguments for friendship. I did not want my ship to be associated with his: the raven had to go. On the other hand, I liked the effect of the pale blue background.

"In that case," said Olaf, my sail-maker, "it makes the job easier and cheaper. I need only replace one black form with another. Leave it to me, my Lord."

I did, and the result was marvellous. Where the raven had previously billowed, wings outspread, reared a black stallion, its hoofs threatening to pound the enemy into the sea. I loved it. Eilaf hated it to the same degree. I could tell by his sneers and whispers and the sidelong glances of his cronies. Trouble was brewing, sure as my name is Ulf. Mother sensed it and referred it to father. I am sure that was the reason why he summoned us both to him before our departure to lecture us, his eyes as hard as two shards of glass.

"Boys, you are now on the verge of manhood. Real men set aside pettiness and childhood rivalries. They dwell on the greater good – the leadership of men, the setting of an example. You two carry my name and honour into the wider world. I expect you to bear it with nobility and worthiness." That hard stare bored into my eyes and those of my brother. It was difficult to meet his gaze with my guilt and failings making me irresolute. I am certain Eilaf felt the same and father must have noticed this. With an impatient tone, he said, "Eilaf, Ulf, take each other's hands. Good, now, swear an oath before Odin," he reached behind him and brought forth an effigy of the god.

"Swear you will eschew treachery all your lives and sustain one another when in need."

"I swear it!" We spoke the words together and while I looked straight at Eilaf, he lowered his head and looked at his feet.

"It is done! Avoid the wrath of Odin. Stay true to your oath and now go with your father's blessing." Thorgils laid a hand on our heads, first Eilaf's then mine. When I gazed up at this gigantic man, the sadness and gravity in his face made him seem suddenly aged. A surge of love and gratitude and a desire to bring glory and lustre to the family name accompanied me out of the hall: I was proud to be Ulf Thorgilsson.

I caught up with Eilaf and threw my arm around his shoulder. He glanced at me, surprised.

"Brother, we must honour father and our oath. Let us be friends."

A moment's silence as if he had to consider an agonising decision, then, "It rather depends on you, doesn't it? You have to show respect, for I am the elder."

"Respect has to be earned, Eilaf," I failed once more, speaking without thought and not in the true spirit of reconciliation but out of defensiveness.

A crowd was waiting at the harbour to send us on our way to

whatever fate lay ahead. I spied Asbeorn disentangling himself from the arms of Lykke, while Gytha stood with mother among the womenfolk. I steered Eilaf toward them and together we bade farewell. The smiles and glances of the young women pleased me and I awakened to the knowledge of my status: a handsome warrior-leader.

With this in mind, I leapt aboard *Sjøhingst* and ordered the men to the oars. Smug, I saw Eilaf and Asbeorn were still not ready. We would be away first, as I wanted.

"Cast off! Push!"

I took the steer-board and the *Sjøhingst* responded at once like the sleek thoroughbred she was. The days of practice paid off as we pulled out into deeper water. The voices of Eilaf and Asbeorn rang across the water exhorting their men to greater effort and diligence.

"Raise the sail!" I bellowed. "Oars inboard!"

For a moment, our headway was lost and our ship wallowed as though time stood still. But the sail filled and the familiar exhilarating forward thrust shuddered along the length of the hull as the vessel lifted her bows and sliced through the sea. The spume in my blood! How I yearned to cross the North Sea to gain my first glimpse of the English coast, to lead men in vengeance for the murder of lovely Gunnhild. But first, we had to cross the Baltic, past Gotland Isle and around the tip of our homeland, down to Heidaby.

With a thrill, I thought of meeting the Forkbeard again and putting my sword to his service. And not only of encountering King Sweyn, but also his daughter, my erstwhile playmate, the pretty Estrid. I thought of her often but not as a companion of childhood games. She would be older, a woman now. Would she still like me? These were my thoughts at the steer-board as the wind ruffled my hair and I began to regret my impulsiveness. I wanted to be first out of the harbour at Upsal, but I had never sailed beyond twenty leagues down the coast. Was I steering a true course? I gazed back at the two straining sails in my wake. One a black raven with outspread wings, the other father's green, writhing dragon on a background of green and yellow stripes. It comforted me to see the two lookouts clinging to their respective figureheads and not gesticulating or indicating ought amiss. For the moment, the pleasing sight of the Swedish coastline sliding past our starboard side confirmed the goodness of my direction. The problem might come when I had to head away from Sweden. Father advised us to at that stage keep a straight course until the isle of Bornholm appeared ahead and then steer due west, that is, straight towards the sun. It was easy enough that far, and afterwards we would be led by Asbeorn in his home waters, which he insisted he knew as well as the contours of Lykke's face. I chuckled at the memory, "If you know Danish waters *that* well, we will have no problems Asbeorn," I had teased. Little did I suspect back then I would outdo him in the wooing of a maid.

6

Like most of the other adults inhabiting the Danish capital, Estrid wore paint around her eyes. The effect was startling. She had chosen a silver-blue shade that enhanced the deep blue of her haunting eyes. Outdoing my imagination, she had grown into a splendid, lithe and flaxen-haired woman. The warmth of her greeting mixed with her flirtatious coyness required me to keep my wits about me in order not to be bested.

Estrid was not the only member of her family to comment favourably on the change in my stature and bearing. None other than King Sweyn complimented me on my transformation into manhood when he welcomed us into his hall.

"Tomorrow," he announced, "the harbour will be crowded with long-ships. Two brothers, Thorkell and Hemming of Jómsborg, will arrive with their men, and many specialised warriors. So, it will be the largest force ever assembled to raid England. There will be two companies," he paused and looked from Eilaf to me, "the brothers will lead their Wends and your men and mine will be led by..." I expected him to say the word '*me*' but he added, "...Eilaf, for he has fought in England and I trust in his worth."

"But, will you not come, Sire?" I blurted, discomforted by shock and the smirk on my brother's face.

King Sweyn looked grim and thoughtful.

"I will not. There is much to be set right here, around our own seas."

"Why so glum, brother?" Eilaf taunted me once we were alone.

"Not so," I replied, "just wondering how we will fare without King Sweyn to keep his Danes under control."

"Do you think me not up to the task?"

"I didn't say that, but–"

"But that is what you meant. Hark! I am your commander and you will obey my orders, setting an example to your men as our father would wish. King Sweyn chose me."

"He did and I will obey him."

Eilaf searched my face for lack of sincerity but I softened my eyes and held his gaze. He nodded and muttered, "That's all right then."

Going my separate way, I came across Estrid, although I doubt it was by chance.

"Did you lose your purse, Ulf?"

By instinct, I checked my belt and found the purse safely attached. In reply to her teasing laughter, I said, "Why ask a question if you know it to be pointless?"

"Oh, but it was not. I wanted to know why you have such a long face. Are you not happy to see me again, Ulf?"

"I-I, of course, Estrid. I missed you so much."

"How much?" She drew so close our faces almost touched. I could smell the faint scent of flowers in her hair. But as I reached to embrace and kiss her, she skipped nimbly out of reach.

"Really? *That* much!"

Her tinkling laugh now began to irritate me, annoyed already by Eilaf's presumption.

"Do you wish to know why I'm in a bad mood?"

"If you choose to confide," she said, transforming her expression from mocking into one of endearing concern.

In a few words, I explained her father's decision and what it meant for me.

"My father must have seen qualities in Eilaf that you do not possess. Give him a chance to prove his worth."

"Eilaf is jealous of me. It is he who needs to value *me*."

"Your friend Asbeorn seems to think you will show the world what a mighty warrior you are."

"So, you've been talking about me?"

She laughed and changed the subject, "Are English women pretty, Ulf?"

"I-I have not made a study of them Estrid, why do you ask?"

Another irritating laugh followed by, "Just that you seem so eager to set off for those shores."

At last, I truly understood her feelings for me.

"I have my duty, Estrid. Were it not so, nothing would take me away from the charms of Heidaby."

I looked at her from top to toe to make my meaning clear.

There was no trace of the tormenting laughter now but with a serious countenance, she took my hand, "Come back safe to me, Ulf," and she squeezed it.

The next day, a ringing cheer woke me. In truth, I had overslept after the bounteous feast provided by the Forkbeard. The cheering came from the waterfront area. Dressed, I headed down to the harbour to join the excited crowd gaping at the vast fleet of long-ships being lashed together to create one endless bobbing platform. I had never seen so many vessels crammed in a mass.

"The Jómsborg fleet is here!" a thrilled Dane stated the obvious, nudging me and grinning.

I shall never forget my first meeting with the Wendish commanders in the Forkbeard's hall. Thorkell remains the tallest man I have ever met – a veritable giant. King Sweyn introduced him, "Eilaf, Ulf, meet Thorkell, known as 'the Tall', and his brother Hemming."

"...And to myself as 'the Not-So-Tall'!" Hemming said.

I liked him at once for his self-depreciation.

There followed a discussion on strategy and Thorkell suggested sailing the next day for England. He would make for the coast of Kent with the aim of occupying the port of Sandwich. Our fleet would join him there. Sweyn's ships were behind on preparations so we agreed to leave Heidaby two days after the Jómsborg company. Two more days with Estrid!

I found her outside the hall, bending over a cauldron.

"What are you doing?"

"Simmering weld for a yellow dye. It's about ready to cool then I'll have to strain it. I have a fancy for a bright yellow gown now the spring is advancing."

"Can I help?"

"If you can spare the time. When it's cool, you can lift the pot, it's heavy for me. The secret to getting a good colour is to add chalk to the simmering."

"Have you seen Thorkell?" I asked, uninterested in details of dyeing cloth. "They call him Thorkell the Tall with good reason."

"Do you not have a nickname, Ulf? Should I choose you one?"

That irritating laugh again!

"Legend tells how my great-grandfather was a white bear. I don't believe it, of course, but I wouldn't mind being named Ulf Bear-Strength or Strong-Bear. Nicknames have to be earned, though, maybe in battle."

"You can begin to earn yours by moving that heavy iron pot close to the cauldron."

I obliged and Estrid held a sieve over it. "Hoist the pot and pour the liquid slowly, Ulf. Check the metal is cool enough to hold."

Lucky I came along. I struggled, staggering a little, to hold the weighty metal container and its contents steady for the time needed to sift the liquid free of the residue of stalks and leaves.

"Ulf Strong-Arm! I shall call you that. You would be useful to have around but you must go."

There was no mistaking the sadness in her voice.

"I will return, Estrid. Do not doubt it."

Did I see a tear in her eye?

"Thorkell departs on the morrow but we remain a further two days."

She gave me a wan smile and with a thrill, I knew that I was not mistaken, and that she loved me. The sentiment was mutual. I gazed at the fine structure of her visage and the soulful expression in the deep blue eyes and my heart leapt. On my return, I would speak with father about the union of our families. A bride's dowry would need to be agreed and my assets established. Negotiations would begin after the English campaign and might take up to a year for a settlement.

"There are preparations to oversee. I must go."

On the morning of our departure, Estrid came to me with the gift of a pendant. From a leather thong dangled a thin section of alder branch and into the wood was burned a bind rune – representing a woman's love for a man.

"Wear this and think of me. Safe return."

She hastily pressed her lips to my cheek before hurrying away. I followed her with my gaze but there was no time to pursue her. My men awaited their orders. Eilaf's ship led the way out of the harbour and although I envied him the leadership, part of me preferred the more relaxing role of obeying directions. That was the illusion I carried across the North Sea. Would that events had proved so simple.

The first realisation that Eilaf intended to make life difficult for me came on our arrival in Sandwich. Thorkell and Hemming had occupied the settlement and our combined fleets filled the bay.

We met with the most important jarls in the Saxon hall to discuss our plans.

"We need to know how strong is the new English fleet," Thorkell said, "we cannot sail out blithely in ignorance."

Hemming spoke for the first time, "I persuaded some details out of one of our English captives. It seems the Saxons saw us coming and have sailed along the coast towards the Isle of Wight. So at least we know where to find them."

Eilaf's lip curled, "We are too strong at sea for the Saxons. We need only to send two ships to ascertain their numbers. I suggest Ulf and Asbeorn take their vessels to gather this information."

"It's a dangerous, if not foolhardy mission," Thorkell cautioned. "Two ships against a fleet?"

"Unless, of course, you are afraid, little brother?" Eilaf sneered.

"I will go, willingly," I reacted to his taunt without thinking.

"Me too," Asbeorn said and I was glad of his support.

"It's settled then," Eilaf smirked, with a vindictive glance at me. "Leave at once and may Odin be with you. We await your news. The success of our expedition depends on your courage, brother. Do not fail us!"

"I shall not."

Asbeorn and I gathered our crews and rowed out to our respective ships, but not before we exchanged opinions.

"Eilaf wants rid of me."

"Nonsense! We need to know the size of the English fleet. It is common knowledge they have increased their numbers."

"It's like walking unarmed into a pack of wolves."

"So, we'll have to be careful."

We sailed along the south coast and the wind seemed to be freshening. One of my thegns, Halvar, confirmed my suspicion.

"Keep an eye on the weather, there's a storm brewing."

I needed no telling, and we had to tack against the north-easterly wind to make progress. Our first sighting, far off, was of a score of English ships. What happened proved so confusing we only made sense of it later. As the sea became more agitated, we stayed at a safe distance from the English, who in any case seemed to be more intent on piracy. They had cut off a number of merchant vessels running for a harbour to flee the increasingly rough waves. Before our unbelieving eyes, the English crews boarded the traders and, without mercy, slew the mariners. Amazed, we watched them throw the bodies into the sea and load the plundered cargo on board their vessels. How could it be possible? The English King's ships attacking and robbing their own merchants?

I ordered our ship into a bay, under the lee of a headland, where we took in our sail and anchored in the more placid water. On the opposite side of the small gulf, the rollers were crashing in long waves and flinging foam ashore in a thunderous din. The sky had become dense with black clouds and rain began to lash down. I was glad to see Asbeorn's ship plunge into our bay to join us. I waved to him to indicate I was going on land. I intended to climb the promontory to keep an eye on the English ships.

This was easier said than done. A track led up the cliff but the rain thrashed into my face and my cloak was soon wet through with the driving wind pressing it into my body. On top of the cape, I struggled to the western side and peered against the rain out to sea, where the massive waves had scattered the plunderers' ships. Or at least, at the time, I believed them the vessels we had seen. But I was wrong. There was about four score of them, pursuing the raiders as it turned out, many driven ashore and wrecked on the rocky coast. The others struggled against the raging seas to keep from being swept to the same doom.

Movement on the coast captured my attention. What was happening? They were slaughtering the survivors who had staggered ashore!

The English were doing our job for us...fighting among themselves. I could make no sense of it. With one last seaward glance to see how the remaining ships were faring, I hurried back down to my waiting rowing boat and returned on board. We decided to wait out the night in the lee of the headland. One of my men drew my attention to a dozen English ships heading eastwards under very light sail. They did not attempt to enter our bay, to my relief.

The storm spent during the night and in the morning when we were ready to leave our anchorage, a spiral of smoke rose from the other side of the headland. Soon it became a dense, billowing cloud.

Calling to Asbeorn, we agreed to investigate. We found the Saxons burning their own ships!

It was days later when we learnt that a Sussex thegn, Wulfnoth, had seduced the crews of twenty ships to betray the fleet and take to piracy. His men conducted the firing of the wrecks. Only when we heard these reports did we understand what we had witnessed. The commanders of the craft surviving the storm prudently sailed them around Kent, avoiding our fleet, and took them to the fortified port of London.

Thorkell, Henning and Eilaf could make no sense of our garbled report. The only thing we were clear on was the weakening of the Saxon fleet. We held a meeting to decide the best course of action. In the end, we decided to accept the frightened offer of three-thousand pounds to leave Kent. An assault on London tempted us but the English defences of the city were too strong. Good sense prevailed. Thorkell led the call to abandon the attack. There was no point in losing vast numbers of men in a long, unrewarding siege when there was rich land to ravage.

I returned to my one pressing desire.

"We should punish Oxford for what they did to Gunnhild and our people." To my surprise, Eilaf was in complete agreement with my suggestion: a rarity.

"We will leave Oxford to you," Thorkell said, "and meanwhile explore the east coast to see what we can cast our eyes upon."

Leaving a force to protect our ships, we marched through the Chiltern hills into the familiar town of Oxford. One of the first build-ings we attacked was the Royal Mint. To our delight, it was stocked with the new silver coinage that Aethelred had ordered for distribution. On the front, the coins bore an image of his head surrounded by his name and on the back, a small cross in the centre. We carried off an enormous sum in oak chests and then torched the building and all those around it until the town was ablaze. Many of the residents escaped into the countryside but we did not pursue them. Instead, we marched either side of the River Thames back to our ships, satisfied with our booty and, in my case, revenge for Gunnhild. The sacking of Oxford brought to an end the campaigning year, so we wintered in Sandwich, paying for food, thus honouring our pact with the Saxons of Kent.

A ship came from Thorkell to propose a new campaign in the spring. Eilaf agreed, so instead of choosing to sail back to Denmark, his fleet joined us to winter in Sandwich. The cold months passed in pleasant company without problems. We discovered that King Aethelred had taken his advisers to the safety of Bath. Our informants advised us that the chief opposition would come from worthier men in East Anglia and Mercia. So, we began to make our plans for the spring. I would not have been so relaxed and happy had I known it would be another two years before I set eyes once more on Estrid. I made do with my pendant which I touched whenever I thought of her, which was often.

7

EAST ANGLIA, SPRING 1010 AD

We sailed into the prosperous port of Ipswich, identified by Thorkell in the autumn for its rich pickings. This thriving centre was defended by an earthwork raised by Danes. Behind the walls, the settlement was laid out in a series of concentric horseshoe-shaped streets. Once we had broken down the gate, the street fighting was ferocious and with our force so large we prevailed and sacked the town. I fought beside Eilaf and Asbeorn and noticed with approval how my brother had grown into a formidable warrior.

With Ipswich in our possession, we gathered in a war council. Some of the older thegns reminded the newcomers of what had happened six years before when our father and the Norse host had been driven back to their ships. The East Anglian Ealdorman, Ulfcytel Snillingr, nearly defeated them.

"I remember, father says it was the most 'deadly hand play' he ever met in England." I said, "he says if this Ulfcytel had not been disobeyed by his men, our army would have been wiped out."

"Are you afraid of him, Ulf?" Eilaf sneered.

"Not at all, I was about to suggest that we hunt him down – conduct a grudge fight. Unless *you* are afraid, Eilaf?"

Thorkell intervened and when he stood to his full height everyone listened.

"We should not squabble among ourselves," he glared at the two of us. "I think Ulf's idea is sound. We ought to strike before this noble warrior has a chance to make us suffer." He rolled out a chart, bending his long frame over to peer at it. "Thegn Edil Keldsson found this and other maps in a church with silver cups and crosses. A good day's work Edil!" He pointed to a place on the map. "This is Thetford, burnt by King Sweyn six years ago. It is a key to the whole area. Look here, shaded in smudged lines to the north-east of the town is the heath of Wretham. If we take those heights first, we can meet on the same battlefield where this Ulfcytel inflicted defeat on the Forkbeard."

Five weeks after disembarking, we lined up in a shield-wall close to the pit at Ringmere. It lay on the heath pointed out by Thorkell. The combined force of East Anglicans and the fyrd of Cambridgeshire led by Ulfcytel was coming up the rise at a steady pace to clash with us. Above the approaching host fluttered a white banner with a red cross. Superimposed on the cross was a blue shield with three golden crowns – the emblem of the once proud kingdom of the East Angles. But these men could not boast the same mettle as their forefathers, with the noble exception of Ulfcytel, whose well-deserved byname, Snillingr, translated as 'the bold'.

When the shield-walls engaged, our pressing was fierce. We had the advantage of the slope and of the oft-reminded grudge to drive us on. The result was the forcing back of the East Anglian contingent and the loss of nerve of the cowardly Thurcytel, known as 'Mare's Head'. However he got that name, the battle turned into a rout with his flight as swift as any mare. The East Angles fled, leaving only the men of Cambridgeshire to stand and fight. Utmost respect was due to them; they fought long and hard but they too broke ranks in the end. I learnt later that I slew King Aethelred's brother-in-law with my axe – a fine warrior. Others of the enemy to fall included the grandson and son-in-law of the famed ealdorman Bryhtnoth.

Our crushing victory paid off the grudge we harboured against Ulfcytel but he had made good his escape to fight another day. Our success, as Thorkell pointed out, gave us control of Thetford whose terrified inhabitants deserted the town. We took what we valued or needed, from what the folk left in their haste to flee. Then we burnt the place to the ground. Too important strategically to leave for the English to reoccupy, it controlled the ancient track from Colchester to Brancaster known as Peddar's Way. The Icknield Way also ran through it, giving access to Cambridge, Hertford, and eventually, London.

Taking advantage of our success, we pressed into north-east Mercia, which now lay open, where we benefitted greatly from this new raiding ground. When we struck south, the fyrd moved north and when we turned west, they hurried east. The witan was summoned to Aethelred to decide how to defend against us but if anything was decided, it did not last a month. The puniness of the enemy rendered our forays much easier. They had no leader who could collect an army, but each fled as best he could. In the end, no shire would help another. I heard a rumour that since our arrival in 1009, in sixteen months we had ravaged fifteen shires. I believe it to be true.

Instead of fighting like Ulfcytel, the English offered us tribute, always too late. After we injured them most and accepted truce and tribute, we journeyed nevertheless in bands everywhere and harried the people of the countryside and small towns, plundering and killing. Our fortunes increased. Three months passed before we decided to turn back to the ships, leaving a trail of destruction behind us. My reputation as a warrior burgeoned with each and every encounter, and with the recounting of my deeds exaggerated, Eilaf grew more bitter.

Our next move was to sail down the coast. It was good to be back aboard *Sjøhingst* after marching the length and breadth of the eastern shires. Thorkell and Eilaf settled on a plan to press into Wiltshire, a rich county close to the heartland of the English King. I think the intention was to extort a much higher tribute in exchange for our departure to Denmark. I hoped this was the idea so I could bear plunder back to Estrid. Among the treasures, jewels and silks we had seized I had selected choice gifts for her.

With so much in our favour it was impossible to conceive, before the Christians' great feast on the eve of winter, of anything going awry. And yet, a self-inflicted disaster was to occur to our combined companies the following year.

With Saxon morale irreparably lost, to all appearances, taking the food and the wealth of the people was like wresting an apple from the hand of a babe. In control of the territory, such was our confidence that I discussed the possibility with Thorkell of persuading the Fork-beard to come to claim the crown of the whole country. There were many in the Danelaw who would welcome him with open arms but also Saxons, elsewhere, who longed for peace and a firm hand. These were the nature of our discussions as we feasted off the fat of the land in the early months of 1011.

The spring brought more raiding and to my dismay, Asbeorn was wounded in a skirmish. We forced a healer, a monk, to tend to him. Luckily, the slash down his chest did not fester and although a rest was enforced, he made a good recovery. His wound came as a reminder of our mortality. The campaign since 1009 had left me without as much as a scratch and I was beginning, in my foolishness, to believe us invincible and untouchable. Indeed, we were, until the events of September. I repeat, our success hitherto was not only due to our prowess in combat but also to treachery and disarray among our foes.

We resumed raiding in Kent. A siege of Canterbury delayed our progress, but once more the English were their own worst enemies. The town was betrayed for coin, the gate flung open and we surged into the narrow streets to wreak destruction. Canterbury proved a suitable base for our winter quarters. Easy to defend and with well-stocked granaries, we made it our home for months.

The new year found us comfortably installed and some of our

men took English women as wives. There was little pressure to return to Denmark with our bellies full and our purses bulging. Our situation changed in April when an English delegation presented itself to Thorkell, Eilaf and the other leaders. Their proposal for our departure from England was the princely sum of forty-eight thousand pounds. Never had such a huge amount been raised as a tribute. The temptation to accept caused little debate among us.

A second factor provoked the forthcoming trouble. When we took Canterbury, we seized an elderly Christian leader called Archbishop Aelfheah. This man was gentle and kind but persistent in trying to persuade us to turn against our gods with strong arguments. Eilaf, in particular, hated him for this since he was particularly devoted to Thor and sacrificed to the god whenever he could.

The problem, which was to cause a series of grave events, was Eilaf's demand for a separate ransom for the archbishop. Some of the Saxons were willing to try to raise the silver but Aelfheah, a stubborn man, refused to countenance it.

"Either find the money or you will die at my hand," Eilaf threatened the hoar-headed man, thrusting his visage into that of the cleric. The latter, sustained by his faith and total unconcern for his own life, continued to defy my brother. Matters worsened until the full moon arrived: a time Eilaf had chosen as a deadline.

"Bring the prisoner out before the whole army," Eilaf said, "I will punish his disobedience myself."

"He is an old man, Eilaf," I said, "there is no honour to be gained, you will only strengthen the English resentment."

"I care nought for what the English think. It is a feeble race with less spine than a jellyfish!"

"I beg you to reconsider."

"Have you no stomach for entertainment?"

"Is that what you call it?"

The argument might have continued but Thorkell the Tall intervened. He pointed at the bound, white-haired prisoner.

"Do you want money, Eilaf? I will give you more than the Saxons can gather for this poor, frail creature. Name your price. I will give you everything I have gained, except my ship."

I gazed at Thorkell in astonishment. Why would he do that? What value did he see in the old man? Thorkell believed in our gods, as did Eilaf and I.

"I don't want your money, friend Thorkell," Eilaf spoke with a respectful tone. He shook his head, "I wish to make an example of those who defy me. Lead him westwards along the river."

Eilaf chose a place known as Greenwich, a port along the Thames famed for its grassy fields. He halted the army there on the meadow. The men were curious to see what one of their leaders intended to do with the captive priest of the hated religion.

Thorkell and I failed in a last attempt to dissuade Eilaf. The flashing fury in Thorkell's eye did not bode well.

A stake was driven into the soft earth and Aelfheah's wrists bound to it, so that he was kneeling in front of the pole.

I seized Eilaf by the wrist, "You cannot do this. Not to an old man. It is too cruel!"

My brother grinned but I could not strike him before the assembly, else one of us would have had to die and I considered that no fair exchange for a skinny old cleric.

"If you have no stomach to watch the spectacle, brother, go hence!"

He shook free his wrist, pulled a dagger from his belt, stepped across to the prelate and sliced away his tunic, revealing his bare back. So I was right. Eilaf meant to spread-eagle the old priest. In our history, it was a hideous death reserved for the most valiant enemy warriors. If they did not cry out in pain they gained admittance at once to Valhalla. This wretch was no warrior but his paradise awaited him after martyrdom. His ribs stood out from his bowed back, making my brother's butchery so much easier. Eilaf carved with his knife either side of the bony man's spine. He cut the flesh back from the ribs and hacked at those bones near the spine with a hand-axe until they were all severed. I believe the poor victim never heard the raucous cheers and shouts of the savage onlookers. Mercifully, his heart must have failed him early in the torture. By the end of this red-spattered operation, the frail body slumped with the two 'wings' spread out behind, like the eagle of its name.

Sickened, I turned away to seek out Thorkell but did not find him. Asbeorn, well recovered from his wound, comforted me.

"Come, Ulf, it is a sorry sight and not fitting behaviour in a warrior. We should find some strong drink."

The old man meant little to me but his importance in my future life cannot be understated. In his insatiable act of vengeance and cruelty, Eilaf had unleashed events which were to affect all our lives.

The defiance of Thorkell led to the single most important conse-quence. When I awoke the next morning, my head thick from drinking to excess, confusion reigned supreme. Men stood in groups with arms waving and voices raised. I caught one of them by the arm, "What's going on?"

"Erik, here, says they've gone."

"Gone? Who's gone?"

"All of them!"

I grabbed the man by the front of his tunic, "Start making sense, now!"

"Thorkell, Lord, with all his crews. None of them's where they should be and their things are gone!"

I gabbled a word of thanks and ran to take a horse. If I rode fast, I could cover the three leagues to Sandwich Bay in an hour. I had to join Thorkell; I wanted to be with him when he told the Forkbeard about our campaign. It was a grave error to leave in haste and confu-sion. No blame can be attached to me for not understanding his plan: unimaginable at the time.

When I arrived within sight of the sea, my heart sank. Too late! They must have set off at first light. So not a spur-of-the-moment decision, but a well-planned move. Bringing my grey mare to a halt, I sat and stared out to sea and began to count the dark shapes bobbing away from land. As I gaped, the oarsmen hauled their oars aboard and the brightly-coloured sails unfurled, filling with the wind, to be made fast. By now, I counted more than forty ships and later confirmed a tally of forty-five. Confused, I watched the lead ship, Thorkell's, veer due south instead of heading north-east for Denmark. It made no sense unless he intended to go raiding further along the south coast on his own.

What Thorkell had in mind was much worse. This tall, magnificent warrior, forsaking friends and allegiances, took his forty-five ships to swear fealty to the enemy – to King Aethelred. The jubilant Saxons were only too pleased to ensure the news reached us in Canterbury as soon as possible.

I sought out Henning, one of the few Jómsborg Wends to remain with us. "Did you know about your brother's plans?" I had difficulty keeping the accusation from my voice.

I'd always liked Henning and now, his sincere, round face grew anxious.

"Eilaf's headstrong and he offended Thorkell with his intransigence. They had heated words again last night over that old priest. I can't understand why Thorkell cared about an enemy of our gods..."

"Me neither, but there it is. And–"

"But to go over to our sworn enemy. I can't believe it of Thorkell. Eilaf must have offended him."

"What are we going to do?"

"King Sweyn will be beside himself with rage when he finds out."

"He will. There are no winners in this tale. As their brothers, we should return with our crews and booty to recount the tale."

"Is that wise, Ulf? You will make an enemy of your brother if you lay the blame for Thorkell's reaction on him."

"Ha! He's an enemy already. Do you not see how he glares and mutters whenever I'm around?"

"Even so, it's unwise. We can't just slip away in the night like Thorkell did. We must call the jarls together to discuss everything, Eilaf included."

The meeting turned out as heated as I feared. A huge vein

throbbed on the forehead of Eilaf when I suggested returning to Denmark.

"Go running back home, little brother. Real men have unfinished business here with those who betrayed us!"

A throaty roar greeted his words with heads nodded in approval.

"There is truth in what you say, brother, but I would advise caution. Is it not better to bring reinforcements over from Denmark? More ships and crews to face Thorkell and the English fleet?"

"Ulf is right." Henning turned to gaze around the excited faces.

"He is not! I say we strike at once against the traitor!"

Eilaf appealed to popular emotions. I could not compete but felt one last argument ought to be used.

"Eilaf, your intransigence over the old priest has cost us dear. Will you repeat your error and lead your men to disaster? Let me fetch King Sweyn."

His eyes flashed, "Run off home, little brother. Leave the fighting to the unafraid!"

"Those who slaughter defenceless old priests?"

I muttered this so low he did not hear – maybe as well. There could have been but one surviving brother if he had.

"Then I will depart with the high tide!" I made my voice resound in the hall.

"I will come with my men," Henning said.

"Me too," Asbeorn declared and I was glad of it.

"We have enough vessels to defeat Thorkell. Three fewer makes no difference." Eilaf's lip curled into a sneer.

"Fifty more ships will not come amiss, either. We'll see what King Sweyn says."

As I looked around the room, I saw the fire extinguish in many eyes and doubt creep over the more experienced countenances.

However, the decision was made and like men who have cast the die, we could not will them to turn back into our palms because the number did not please us.

8

HEIDABY, OCTOBER 1012 AD

More than three years had passed since our departure for England but now our ships nosed into Heidaby harbour and tied up at the jetty. I, the young, inexperienced steersman who had taken us out of the port back then, stood tall and proud scanning the cheering crowd, which was gathering faster than the eye could blink. And there she was! Estrid, standing among her people on tiptoe waving a yellow kerchief in the air. My sight, battle- and sea-trained, proved too keen to miss the one person I wished to see above all others.

A prodigious leap took me from the steer-board at the stern onto the jetty. I could have broken a leg as I slithered on the fish slime coating the wooden boarding, such was my eagerness to be ashore.

"I was the first to see the three sails," she said breathlessly when I forced my way to her.

"Ask me how I am," I teased.

"You seem well enough, judging by how you leap around."

"And you?"

"Fine. I have a surprise for you but you will need to come to the Hall."

"One moment. Let me give orders."

I roared a series of commands, hushing the crowd and impressing those nearest me with the depth of my voice. The war chests had to be carried to King Sweyn. My gifts for Estrid were in one. She seemed eager to be off, so I hesitated only briefly in making sure my orders were being obeyed. Satisfied, I hurried after her, admiring her straight back and the alluring sway of her hips. She turned round to make sure I was with her and, reassured, she favoured me with a smile I'd dreamt about for three years. She linked her arm under mine and tugged, "mmm, Ulf Strong-Arm," she said appreciatively, "Come on!"

"You seem in a wondrous hurry. Are the Norsemen coming?" I joked.

For a moment she looked serious, "You can see the new fortifications father has strengthened in your absence but not the new alliances he has forged." If possible, her expression grew graver, "Oh, Ulf, whatever happens in the Hall, promise you will not be angry with me."

"My love, why should I be angry with you?"

"I hope you will not be," she squeezed my hand.

We still had not kissed and when I tried to pull her to me, she squirmed away.

"Later!" she laughed, "if you are not furious with me, that is."

"Isn't furious *worse* than angry?"

We arrived at the King's Hall, where she slipped into the flame-lit interior. The smoke-filled air was heavy with scents, spices and smoke. After two days at sea, my lungs rebelled and I coughed.

"Come!" she hissed as insistently as before. Even in the gloom of the hall, there was no mistaking the seated figure of the fork-bearded monarch.

"Sire," I bowed.

"Father, Ulf has come – with two other ships! Isn't it wonderful?"

"Only two ships?"

"Three, Sire." I said.

"Why so few?"

"A disaster, my Lord."

"Why, has there been a storm? Did we lose our ships?"

I shook my head.

"What then, did we suffer defeat in battle?"

"We won all our battles and skirmishes. In the process, we gathered endless riches."

"That's hardly a catastrophe...although...for the English..." Sweyn chortled. "I think you'd better explain yourself."

I regretted not having waited for Henning and Asbeorn, but Estrid had been in such a hurry to fetch me to the Hall. I began an explanation of the events at Greenwich while Estrid, agitated and impatient, wrung her hands.

"So, let me get this right," Sweyn said, "your brother and Thorkell quarrelled over a matter of principle. The pair of idiots argued over a Christian priest."

I had to admit to the folly of it.

"Not just any priest, Lord. An important one!"

"Is that why your brother spread-eagled him?"

"For refusing to pay to save his miserable life."

"I can understand it might be termed a disaster for the elderly archbishop and that the English will not have taken kindly to this treatment of their prelate. But I wouldn't call it such, Ulf."

"Will it suit for the loss of Thorkell and forty-five ships, Sire?"

"Eh?"

"Thorkell swore allegiance to King Aethelred."

"By Thor, he did! And did Aethelred accept it, knowing he would incur my wrath?"

"I'm afraid he did, Lord, which is why I hurried home to bring the news." Now the Forkbeard swore under his breath, discomfited. "There's more: Eilaf will not be restrained. I urged him to await your coming to unite forces and destroy the traitor. But he would not be held back."

"The idiot! if he survives, he will answer to me for his foolhardy actions."

King Sweyn pinched and pulled at his bottom lip.

"Father! Will you not give my news to Ulf? I'm bursting with it!"

The ruler frowned at his daughter. At last, he showed signs of controlling his temper. Was that not a smile replacing the thunder on his brow?

"Your father is more than a friend, Ulf. He is a *true* friend. Happily, he is a frequent and most welcome visitor to my Hall. We spoke of uniting our two families while you were away..."

"I couldn't help but overhear them, Ulf. I was serving at father's table. So I told them we loved each other. You don't mind, do you?"

I kept my face expressionless.

"Mind?" I said, "I'm damned furious!"

Estrid did not notice me wink at her father and her face was a picture. "Oh, Ulf!"

We burst out laughing together, Sweyn and I.

"What beasts you men are!" she protested.

"Lord, what do *you* say to this proposal?"

"I was unaware of a proposal, Ulf."

"W-well, no. I-I...there's been no time."

"Do you not think you'd better ask for Estrid's hand? Do you want to take her for wife?"

I sank to my knees before the King of Denmark.

"Do I have your consent to wed Estrid, Lord?"

My heart beat more fiercely at that moment than when the enemy was advancing on our shield-wall.

"Not only my consent, my boy, but also my blessing! The dowry is agreed with your father and you are made jarl in Sweden with land and people of your own."

"What a homecoming!"

The radiance of my expression made Estrid throw herself at me to receive my first kiss from a woman. I hoped my inexperience would not betray me.

"That's settled then, you will wed at the winter solstice, the nearest Frigga's Day to Jul."

Jul was ten days before the end of the year according to the Christians' calendar – at least that was something useful the Christians offered us – a better almanac. But Jul was so soon! Three moons hence and I still did not know the woman!

Distracted, I realised Sweyn was still talking, "...right away. Bring them all here for the festivities."

He was referring to my family. "Anyway, we cannot take a fleet to England until the spring–"

King Sweyn broke off at the sound of a number of heavy chests being dropped on the floor.

"Ah, the spoils!"

I lifted a ring of keys from my belt and began to unlock and throw back one lid after another. The principal contents were masses of silver coins. King Sweyn's eyes lit with pleasure, not greed.

"My gift to you, Sire. I beg you to leave me only the small locked chest remaining."

"And what lies therein, Ulf?"

"Gifts for my bride, Lord."

"Ooh! let me see! Let me see!" Estrid chirped.

"Carry this to the Lady's chamber!"

But I held on to the key; the chest was locked.

Out of the corner of my eye, I saw Asbeorn arrive and kneel before the King.

"Odin bless you, Sire. I beg your indulgence."

"How so?"

"Only you can grant my request, Lord."

Now I listened with ardour. Asbeorn kept no secrets from me. What did he want of his King?

"Lord, my woman, Lykke, is at Upsal and I wish to marry."

So that was it!

"Can you provide for her as you ought, Asbeorn?"

"Sire, I return with a chest of silver. The rest I must give to Ulf's father and his crew."

"That is fairly said, lad! You may wed on the same day and at the same place as your friend."

We embraced and had it not been for the dark cloud of Eilaf's behaviour hanging over me, I swear I would have been the happiest man on Earth.

Our two ships sailed into Upsal on the first day of settled weather. The felicitations received for my forthcoming wedding made the reunion with my family sweeter.

Father explained what had been happening during my absence from my homeland.

"Do you think you are the only one who's been enjoying himself knocking enemies on the head, Ulf? Did King Sweyn not speak to you at all about our victories? No? Here, sit. A drink? It's like this: King Sweyn and our King Olof Skötkonung attacked the Norwegians. We were tired of their depredations and decided to conquer Norway once and for all. We won a crushing battle at Svolder, Ulf...let me tell you about it." My father spoke at length about the glorious deeds of that day and his part in the victory. When, at last, he had recounted every last detail, I asked, "Who now rules over Norway?"

"The Forkbeard divided the country up and the Danish Jarl of Lade, Eric son of Heakon, occupies the Norwegian throne. He's King in all but name. Sweyn nominated him...regent. It keeps the Norwegians more malleable, is my guess." Father looked at me; I knew that expression, it meant he had been withholding a surprise. "When King Sweyn divided up the Norwegian territory, he kept his closest and dearest in mind. Before you sail back to Heidaby, don't you think you should visit your new lands in Trøndelag, Jarl Ulf?"

"The King did mention something about a jarldom for me but I did not press him on it."

"Then you must go at all costs. You will not have thanked him enough. It is a magnificent gift, Ulf! Trøndelag is central to the country and one of the most fertile regions in the land. It also boasts a long coast, so you can sail out on raids to your heart's content!" Father warmed to his argument, "The men of Trøndelag are sturdy warriors and will follow a noble leader to the ends of the Earth."

"So, do you think they will accept an outsider?"

"When they hear you marauded through England and are wedded to the daughter of King Sweyn, they will throw themselves at your feet!"

"Father, you exaggerate!"

Our conversation between father and son lasted until the shadows grew long and I revelled in the company of the man I idolised, which had been denied me for three years. I kept the shade on my heart from him. No point in destroying father's happiness with bad thoughts about Eilaf. At least, not for the moment. To my immense joy, he agreed to ride with me to Trøndelag. There, everything proved to be as promised. My new people did not regard me with suspicion or hostility but with a natural reserve, which I intended to overcome when I brought my bride among them. Estrid would win their hearts as she had mine. Of that I was certain.

The voyage back to Heidaby was tedious because the womenfolk made my head spin with their arrangements for the wedding. Why did they have to complicate everything so?

Nonetheless, I was grateful for their presence in the period leading up to the feast of Jul. Gytha and mother spent their time with an increasingly nervous and snappy Estrid. Whatever I said and did irritated her and it was only Asbeorn's calm and stolid nature that stopped me from quarrelling with her. It got me through to the period when the two men to be wed and the two women went their separate ways as tradition demanded. Thus, we could strip away our former selves before entering our new lives together. As I said to Asbeorn, "I hope Estrid strips away her unpredictable moods!"

"She's worried lest ought go wrong on her big day, is all."

"Today, she's stripped off her old clothing and the kransen, the coronet symbol of her virginity."

"I expect you'll see the matter to its conclusion as soon as possible, Ulf," Asbeorn winked.

For a moment I did not understand his meaning, such was my innocence in matters concerning men and women.

Meanwhile, Estrid and Lykke, attended by their mothers, sisters and married female relatives and friends were cleansed in a bathhouse. Estrid told me afterwards what happened there: they placed hot stones in a tub to make steam and the two brides were switched with birch twigs to make them perspire. Supposedly it washed away their maiden status. Estrid made light of the switching, but the plunging into freezing water afterwards to close the pores shocked her.

Asbeorn and I had to undergo rituals too. Attended by our fathers and Asbeorn's married brother, we took our parts in the symbolic sword ceremony. In my case, they had broken into a grave and laid my grandfather's sword by the skeleton of a warrior. Of course, it should have been my grandfather's grave with his mortal remains, but he lay far away in Sweden so they lent me one of King Sweyn's ancestors. My task involved entering the grave and retrieving the weapon at night. In so doing, I symbolically entered death as a boy and emerged into life as a man. I had seen much worse than an ancient dusty skeleton while on the battlefields of England – but one must honour tradition. After obtaining the blade, I went to join Asbeorn in the bath house to wash away my bachelordom and purify myself for the wedding ceremony.

Asbeorn is my friend but he annoyed me by laughing at my innocent questions when father tried to explain my husbandly duties.

There were no more preparations to be made. Thor's day was complete; the morrow, Frigga's day would see us wed. Great care was lavished on the hair of the two brides the following morning. Both young women had long, wavy blonde locks and they emerged wearing their bridal-crowns, which replaced the simple gold circlets of the kransen. The crowns, instead, were made of silver adorned with rock crystals and had elaborate designs of clover leaves, draped with red and green garlanded silk cords. Estrid had added a finishing touch by weaving in some ears of wheat. I tried not to gape like an idiot at her beauty.

We men had no special dress but we carried our newly-acquired swords, and since my favourite god is Thor, I also hefted a hammer. Apart from any other reason, the hammer is symbolic of mastery in the union and old folk insisted it would ensure a fruitful marriage.

I believe Estrid's snappy moods leading up to the ceremony induced me to carry that heavy tool to the rite. I did not want to risk her taking charge of me! As it turned out, I need not have worried. A more respectful and happier relationship is impossible for me to imagine. With the wisdom of years, I now see the perfect marriage, mine, as one where respect, sacrifice and love are given willingly in equal measures by both parties. Instead, that day, I stood there a glowering fool with my heavy hammer weighing me down.

The ceremony began with the exchange of dowry and *mundr* – the bride price – before witnesses. This concluded, and the gods and goddesses were summoned. We sacrificed a sow to Freyja, its blood collected in a bowl, fir twigs dipped in and sprinkled over Estrid and me. Now the time had come for me to present the ancestral sword to Estrid. This she would keep for our firstborn son, should the gods grant this blessing. Estrid unbuckled a sword she carried at her waist; how could her father's protection be better symbolised? On the hilts of the exchanged swords, we each placed a wedding band of gold for the other to wear, to consecrate the union. All that remained was for me to race Asbeorn into King Sweyn's Hall for the feast. Whoever lost the race had to serve beer to the other throughout the evening. None of my contemporaries was as swift of foot as me, so Asbeorn, as I expected, was condemned to an evening of servitude. I then blocked the doorway to the Hall as custom demanded so that Estrid could not cross the threshold without my assistance. Thus, she completed her symbolic journey from maidenhood to marriage. As I carried her through the doorway, she whispered, "Don't forget the ceiling."

I had not forgotten. The very last rite was to plunge my sword into the ceiling. I am endowed with a warrior's strength and to general acclaim, the blade plunged deep into the wooden ceiling. The deeper it enters, the longer the relationship will endure. The most satisfied face in the room at the blow belonged to Estrid.

"Let the feasting commence!" King Sweyn's voice rose above the clamour.

9

HEIDABY, WINTER 1012-1013 AD

Azure skies feathered by wispy mares' tails, showing neither intent nor portent, deceived us into thinking there were no menacing storm clouds gathering elsewhere that winter. I remember those months as idyllic: the happiest of my life. They included driving my body through extremes, from the tenderness of Estrid's embraces to marrow-chilling swims across the harbour, muscle-searing wrestling with Asbeorn, and hours of combat practice. We carried our purpose to excessive lengths but it paid off in terms of battle readiness.

In those days, you didn't need to be a seer to know that war was in the offing. One glance at King Sweyn's outraged countenance was enough. Only a deaf and blind man might have been excused ignorance of the bellicose preparations occupying the smithies and shipyards of Heidaby for long hours.

I learnt much later that while I frolicked with my newly-wed bride, overseas my brother had found himself a mistress. This woman was to save his life but this I will relate in due course. It's fair to say my brother and I had not always been on the best of terms, but I admit Eilaf was always a good-looking rascal. The maids of Upsal were ever given to giggles, nudges and fluttering lashes in his presence. That he made no conquests among them I'm sure depended on lack of interest on his part. Remember how young we were when we went off to fight in England? Now it was time to do so again.

King Sweyn, so esteemed for the rapidity and precision of his movements, surprised us all by not risking the direct crossing to the Humber estuary. I told him the men of the Danelaw would welcome a Danish king with open arms, but he landed at Sandwich. There, he waited for stragglers to re-join the fleet before sailing up the east coast into the choppy brown waters of the Humber. I could only guess that his diversion to Kent was to gather news from his informants; anyway, we disembarked twenty miles up the Trent at Gainsborough in Lindsey. The reception he received proved the accuracy of my prediction. Sweyn did not have to leave that settlement to be accepted as King by the leading men of much crucial territory. Northumbria, Lindsey, the confederation of the Five Boroughs, and the whole of Danish England south of the Welland and east of Watling Street submitted to him.

I can only explain what happened next by pointing to the toll our three-year harrying of the English must have had on their morale. King Sweyn called a moot and after he secured the submission of the leading men by taking hostages, he demanded horses and provisions from them. He then led us out for the reduction of the shires still faithful to Aethelred.

As we proceeded, I wondered what had become of my brother and of Thorkell. I would not have long to wait to discover it, given our swift progress. In his wisdom, the Forkbeard did not allow us to plunder the countryside until we crossed Watling Street and entered English Mercia. The panicked gabbling of folk fleeing their homes into the towns must account for Oxford and Winchester surrendering as soon as we appeared before their walls. Like the rest of the men, I yearned to wield my axe in wrath. Wherein the honour in taking silver from cowering enemies?

Our King held the whole of the Danelaw, the eastern shires of

English Mercia, and central Wessex through hostages. Now he turned his attention from Winchester to a direct assault on London.

Our scouts reported a citizen garrison supported by Thorkell with his ships' crews and King Aethelred with his personal retainers, and this drove Sweyn into a blind rage. A combination of circumstances interwove to save Thorkell from the horrible fate Sweyn Forkbeard had in mind for him. We reached the Thames at its lowest ebb to take the town of London by surprise and the King's advisers persuaded him to send a detachment to ford the river. Local knowledge of tides is indispensable in such contexts and frankly, we did not possess it. Luckily, Sweyn kept me by his side and did not consign that troop to my command. I confess that sickened by inactivity, it irritated me at the time, but as we gazed, helpless, on the emerging calamity, I thanked the gods for my escape. Our horsemen were halfway across the ford when the tide rushed in like a treacherous assailant catching them unawares. Burdened with weapons and armour, they had no chance of survival as their mounts lost their footing and swam for shore in panic.

How many men drowned I cannot be sure but King Sweyn, a believer in omens, determined that the attack on London was ill-starred. He decided not to besiege the town but to complete the reduction of Wessex. A wiser king than my wife-father I have yet to meet. Another, blinded by a quest for revenge on Thorkell and Aethelred, might have insisted on a lengthy, wearisome siege but Sweyn found a better way to bring down his enemies.

We marched through Wallingford to Bath where he received the submission of the western thegns and where I reunited with my brother. Eilaf, to my amazement, greeted me as a long-lost sibling should. Much as I would like to think it came out of brotherly affection, my more rational mind nagged me that he needed my support for fear of Sweyn's reactions. He required an intermediary to explain his actions after our departure for Denmark. I had left him declaring his avowed intent of taking vengeance on Thorkell.

Over copious amounts of ale, he related his tale of events in my absence.

"The Jómsborg men, without the leadership of Hemming, were not prepared to strike against their own fellows. This left me with no choice but to seek alternative courses of action. I filled my time ravaging the Wessex countryside and capturing small settlements, enough to keep my men satisfied. What else could I do?"

I nodded in understanding of his predicament. Reassured I was not judging him unfavourably, he continued.

"During this time, more and more murmuring grew against King Aethelred and his unjust taxes and actions. Uprising was imminent when, imagine my surprise, none other than Thorkell the Tall sought me out."

"Thorkell! Did he not fear you would slay him?"

"He came under the white banner, Ulf. Try to see my position. How could I move against Aethelred with my reduced numbers and Thorkell playing on his sway over the Jómsborg men? Had I set my face against him, they'd have joined him in a trice. And he knew it."

"So what did he propose?"

"He came with an offer of silver from King Aethelred for every man in exchange for entering his service."

"As mercenaries?"

"That's it."

"And you agreed?"

"What else could I do?"

"So why aren't you in London with Aethelred, now?"

"Thanks to Beornwyn."

"Beornwyn?"

"She's my mistress. I know now that Aethelred sent her to seduce me so she might to spy on me and report to him. The Saxon King did not expect her to fall in love with me. To get to the point, the idea of hiring us paid off for Aethelred. For fear of our strength, the restlessness the King so dreaded died down. That's when he decided he didn't need to pay us anymore. But how could he get away with that?"

Eilaf stared into my eyes and poured himself another ale.

"What happened?"

"Beornwyn is loyal to me and she came all a-tremble. The sly, treacherous cur, Aethelred, planned to slaughter me and massacre all our men in the dead of night. Thanks to my woman, we were ready for them and slew enough of them to send the others packing to the one who commanded the deed. Of course, Aethelred denied all knowledge of the plot and promised to punish the perpetrators but as you might guess, nothing came of that."

Eilaf seized my wrist, "Ulf, we have done nothing wrong. Agreeing to take Aethelred's money bought us time as we awaited your arrival with King Sweyn. He wants to see me in the morning. Will you speak to him in my defence?"

So that accounted for his brotherly affection.

"Of course, I will. My wife-father will be sure to welcome you and your men into our company."

"Wife-father?"

"I wed Estrid."

His face portrayed a range of conflicting emotions. Why could he not be the fond brother he pretended to be when it suited? At last he mastered his feelings, jumped to his feet and embraced me.

"I wish you joy and sons, brother."

The words were fair enough but I would have been a fool to trust Eilaf.

"I will speak with King Sweyn on your behalf."

It was easily done. Eilaf being my brother and Thorgils's son was enough for Sweyn in the absence of blatant treason. In addition, the numbers Eilaf brought to ours were welcome.

The next morning, the Forkbeard commanded Eilaf to retrieve his ships and take them to Gainsborough, where we would join him later by marching our men across central England. The sight of such a mighty host reinforced the growing sentiment throughout the nation that King Sweyn was King in all respects. On our way to Gainsborough, news came that London offered submission. This deprived King Aethelred of his last stronghold. Escape from his lost kingdom, by a touch of irony, depended on the good faith of Thorkell the Tall and his ships. Indeed, we learnt that King Aethelred was quailing aboard Thorkell's ship, where he remained until the important Christian feast of Christ's Mass. They say he sent his Queen, Emma, to her father in Normandy for her safekeeping. When we arrived in Gainsborough, they told us Aethelred had fled to join her, leaving Sweyn in military possession of the whole land.

Eilaf and I were speculating what the Forkbeard would do about Thorkell. For sure, it had to be his next step, when on 3 February 1014 the unthinkable happened. King Sweyn, at the height of his powers, died. Our doom is writ; if I don't die in battle, the best I can hope for is a swift, unexpected and suffering-free end such as the Norns reserved for my wife-father.

While we were away in the south, Sweyn had left his younger son, Cnut, in charge of the ships. So, it was natural the fleet gave its allegiance to him upon the announcement of the King's death. Cnut was an inexperienced commander and this was to cost us dearly. In fairness, we were not ready for a new campaign and the English, emboldened by the death of the Forkbeard, acted at once.

They sent a delegation to Normandy to open talks for Aethelred's restoration. The negotiations could only proceed if Aethelred agreed to be a true lord and rule justly. He swore to forgive everyone for what they had done or said against him. The first we knew of this came in mid-April when he raised a force to lead an expedition against us in Lindsey.

What happened next will remain forever a stain on Cnut's name. He had an understanding with the men of Lindsey by which they agreed to supply his army with horses and join it in a concerted raid on Aethelred's country. But the swiftness of the English force, marching before our preparations were complete, caught us by surprise. Cnut, Eilaf and I had a heated argument. I put it down to

Cnut's inexperience of independent command but, against our recommendation, he decided to withdraw from England. To us, it smacked of unreasonable fear and betrayal. We wanted to fight; not to be seen as cowards.

Worse was to follow. He sailed down the coast to Sandwich, where to my disgust, at Thanet, he set on shore the hostages who had been given to his father and ordered their noses and hands to be cut off. This act of savagery served no purpose in my opinion, but unable to intervene I was left with my own thoughts and regrets. How sorely we missed King Sweyn. The most terrible result of Cnut's ill-judged decision was to leave the men of Lindsey helpless and exposed to the wrath of Aethelred. Word of Cnut's treachery to his allies spread far and wide. I often wonder who the men of Lindsey hated more: Aethelred or Cnut. In Denmark, Sweyn's eldest son, Harald, became King. For Cnut's fortune, Harald enjoyed the support of great men and thanks to one of them, this would later compensate for his weakness as a commander. At least it meant my involvement in England would conclude in a more satisfactory manner. For the moment, I was happy to return home to my bride.

10

TRØNDELAG AND UPSAL, 1014 - 1015 AD

I returned to my beloved Estrid with my mind in a turmoil. Cnut's betrayal of the men of Lindsey weighed heavily upon me. I needed to share my feelings with somebody and in the absence of Asbeorn, who had gone back to Upsal, who better than Estrid? So I thought, yet she did not understand my scruples and did not attempt to improve my black moods which were made worse by her lack of comprehension. Was she trying to defend her brother's cowardly behaviour or simply diminishing the importance of my qualms? Either way, the risk of souring our marriage over my principles proved so real that I decided I would deal with my obsession elsewhere.

I made the choice to leave Estrid in Trøndelag to shake her out of the complacent belief I would adore her regardless of differences on matters of principle. The rectitude of my upbringing meant I placed values at the heart of trust. To love Estrid on my terms, I needed to have faith in her and to do this required the certainty that she was not like her brother. I began to question the haste of our betrothal and in a state of total confusion, took my leave of her. The hurt in her eyes tugged at my heart but, resolute, I headed overland to Upsal, to the wisest man I knew – my father.

The joy of my father at receiving me back from campaigning in England was tempered by how well he knew my moods.

"What ails you, boy?" he asked as soon as we sat alone to savour wine shipped from Heidaby, a fine gift from King Harald's warehouses.

I tried to give a reasoned account of the events leading up to our departure from Gainsborough, careful not to include my own sentiments. My father listened carefully and his face became grim at the implications of Cnut's betrayal for the fate of the men of Lindsey. When I spoke of the mutilation of the hostages, he slammed down his drinking horn and uttered an oath under his breath.

Ever practical, he seized my arm, "Is that why your wife is not with you? Tell me you have not quarrelled."

The anxious tone of his question took me by surprise, but then I had been away on campaign and knew little of the politics of the region.

I shook my head, "Not argued, but Estrid has experienced my ill-humour over this matter."

"You are right to take it hard. No doubt of that. But you must not risk offending King Harald by upsetting his sister. Harald is as like Cnut as an eagle is to a sparrow."

All this while, he clung on to my arm as if to ensure I would not drift away from what he wanted of me. So great was my respect for my sire that there was little danger of such an outcome. His next words aided to clarify my thinking.

"Moral courage, Ulf, is not something that blows in the wind or changes with the weather. It is within a man. It is the decisive factor determining character. Looking inside yourself and drawing upon it means you will ever do what is right. The doing is more important than the knowing." He accompanied these words with a squeeze of my arm, which he at last released.

"Can I ever trust Cnut?"

The flash in the eye of Thorgils Sprakalägg underlined the foolishness of the question.

"These are dangerous times, my lad. The only person you should trust is yourself. The *only* one! We all inherit the capacity for loyalty but not the use to which we should put it. There is the root of your unhappiness: you desire to be loyal to your leader but you do not wish to serve what is petty and vile."

I made no reply, preferring to dwell on the wisdom of these words. Although I knew it not at the time, they would shape my fate and lead to my doom.

With my head clearer, I stayed to enjoy pleasant days with my family and friends until I felt ready to return to Estrid. I found her in a state of considerable unease, which I ascribed to our earlier differences of opinion. This proved only in part correct. She spoke to me of serious events that had occurred during my absence.

"Oh, Ulf, can it be you know nothing of what goes on in your own lands? Olaf Haraldson is proclaimed by the Thing supreme King of Norway according to law in the Uplands. The *bondes*, the leaders, swore oaths to accept him as their King. He grows in strength, Ulf, Earl Hakon gave him his possessions in the Throndhjem country. Do you even know where that is, pudding head?" She gazed at my vague stare with exasperation, "It's the Orkadal, Gaulardal, Strind and Enya district."

"They are just names to me, Estrid. You know I have had no time to explore this land. England is more familiar to me than Norway although in name, Norway is my home. Should I be concerned about this King Olaf?"

"Husband, we should be *most* anxious. The lands to the north and the south have submitted to him. It is only a matter of time before he sets his mind on our territory. You too must bend the knee to him."

"If he guarantees the laws and rights given by King Olaf Trygvason, I see no problem in that."

"Oh, my dear innocent spouse! You *see* no problem! That is because your head is ever far away in other lands. Do you not know that King Olaf Haraldson is a fervent Christian and has vowed to stamp out what he calls *paganism* from Norway? One of the reasons we were so well received in Trøndelag is that we are not Christians and we let our people worship in the sacred groves."

"Do you mean this Olaf will attack us and our folk because we worship the old gods?"

"At last, you follow me, husband!"

"I am not a devout adherent of the wise men but it will be difficult to renounce Odin."

"It was not hard for my grandsire Harald Bluetooth to bring Christianity to Denmark."

"Why then, Estrid, are you not a Christian?"

"Because my father rebelled against my grandsire and used eliminating Christianity and restoring the old gods as an excuse to seize power. Later he changed and welcomed missionary bishops from England, but never imposed baptism on me, more's the pity. It would have been useful now. Ulf, the world is becoming Christian. The old gods are being swept away. Is it not proof the one God of the Christians is more powerful?"

"Or it means those who wield arms in his name are mightier."

"It amounts to the same thing, don't you understand? We also must convert, Ulf."

That was too much. I liked my wife to have spirit but I would not have her command me, even for my own well-being.

I stormed out of the hall and threw myself on the bed to think about what Estrid had told me. Even to my mind, something needed to be done. If this King Olaf had made such progress in gaining lands and men, the menace was real. Around Norway, soon preparations would be made for the great Yule feast. This festival was also a major event for Christians. How we were seen to celebrate it would announce to the world where our faith lay. But assuming I decided to embrace Olaf's religion, how would my people take it? Would I have to force them to convert? What was the purpose of a ruler other than to act in the best interests of his folk to keep them safe and prosperous?

These tormenting thoughts preyed upon my mind until Estrid came into the chamber, and the sweetness of her smile and the beauty of her concern-filled eyes made me decide. What future was there for us in Trøndelag if I took up arms against a mighty ruler? I envisaged a life in the hall with Estrid's children at my knees and a comfortable existence enjoying the fruits of my conquests.

"Where can we find a priest to baptise us, Estrid?"

My wife's comely face lit up with joy, "Oh, you are sensible, Ulf. I love you so much!"

I leant over, took her in my arms and kissed her.

"Strange way to answer my question, sweetness."

"Send to my brother's court with the message that you require a bishop, with all haste, to convert us and the people of Trøndelag. Word will spread of such an important conversion and is sure to reach King Olaf and make of him our friend. Oh, I do love you, Ulf!"

Before the month of Ylir, the Christians' November, a Benedictine monk named Sigefrid arrived. Originally from England, he had since become a bishop and resident at King Harald's court. I took at once to this lean, white-haired gentle man. His quiet conviction and wisdom, ideal to unbend my rigid character, ensured he made rapid progress in interesting me in his beliefs, and of course, Estrid was more amenable. He came with a wonderful reputation, having traversed all parts of Sweden, preaching, baptizing and converting the people to the faith of Christ, and he also urged those who he had imbued with the faith by holy admonitions that they should persevere, for they would receive eternal rewards from God. In particular, he constructed churches, ordained clerics and gave them orders to gain people for the Lord by preaching and baptizing. This was how he succeeded in converting the most hostile heathens. How, then, could such a man fail among us?

I used persuasion to convince my leading thegns. This did not prove as difficult a task as I had feared. Good sense prevailed as each considered what he would lose by defying me, but more importantly by defying King Olaf. Many of the women flocked to listen to Bishop Sigefrid. Despite his strong accent, he had a surprising command of their language and such fine rhetoric aimed in simple terms to the advantage of their understanding ensured that they soon embraced his faith. Of the menfolk clinging to their old beliefs, none had the courage or effrontery to flaunt their amulets or voice their resentment. This was just as well because I had decided to expel any stiff-necked recalcitrants from Trøndelag. It proved unnecessary; instead, a crowd gathered to watch us step naked into the freezing waters of the fjord to be submerged by the goose-pimpled prelate in his linen tunic.

Whether or not my sins had been truly washed away, I emerged with a lightness of being and a sensation of strength of character new to me. I did not fear Odin's wrath because, as Bishop Sigefrid assured me, faithful service to my God would guarantee a spiritual shield in this life and eternity in the next.

All that needed to be verified was what welcome might await me from King Olaf Haraldson.

11

TRØNDELAG, 1015-1016 AD

My new religion taught me humanity is made up of sinners in need of salvation. Christianity credits those who believe with Christ's own righteousness – and that satisfied me. Although I adopted this creed for political reasons, I soon found myself convinced by its strong moral arguments.

This proved to be of fundamental importance even before the Christ's Mass. A messenger arrived from Throndhjem fjord, where King Olaf had taken his ships, bearing a summons to join the monarch there to celebrate that sacred event. I discussed this with Estrid, who pleaded with me to swallow my pride and obey. I was loathe to leave the warmth of my hall to brave the bleak season, but the pointlessness of offending Olaf set me on my way north.

Yuletide was in the offing but my expectations of carousing interspersed with prayer were misplaced. This soon became apparent when I stepped aboard King Olaf's ship. Not many men are taller than me but Olaf's blue eyes were level with the top of my head as he greeted me. I supposed him to be a brawny, broad-shouldered man from his reputation as an indomitable warrior. Instead, he stood thick of waist and muscular, with a head crowned by dark golden curls and beard to match. The force of his personality and warmth of his greeting struck me at once.

"They say you are battle-hardened in England. Is it so?"

"It is, Sire."

"Come then, I have a gift for you."

Olaf led me to the back of his ship and gestured to a fellow who leapt up from the large chest he was sitting on.

"Eric, find the right size for Lord Ulf."

The man picked up a ribbon and moved behind me where he stretched the tape from the outside of one shoulder to the other. What was happening?

"I'll leave it to you, Eric," the King said. "Come, Lord Ulf, let me show you my handiwork." He led me, somewhat perplexed, to the prow of the long-ship where he pointed to the carved figure of a king wearing a crown.

"What do you think?"

I might have expected a ferocious dragon or the ever-popular raven's head. A moment's reflection urged me to dismiss such pagan thoughts. I was standing next to a Christian king after all.

"Did you carve it yourself, Lord?"

"I did."

I leapt on the gunwale and grasped the figurehead to inspect it from close quarters. The precise and intricate carving of the crown would have done credit to any Norse master craftsman.

"Well?"

"It is finely wrought, my King."

Olaf laughed and clapped me on the back with such vigour I feared I may lose my grip and end in the icy waters of the fjord. The King reached up, and offered his hand to help me down beside him.

"Let's see if that wastrel Eric has done my bidding. Come and admire your gift, Ulf!"

Lying on the chest in the stern was a ring-mail coat of the finest workmanship.

"There, what do you think? Eric, lend a hand to put it on!"

The armour weighed on my shoulders but fitted to perfection. The protection it afforded would turn away spearheads, swords and axe blades.

"It's a magnificent gift! Wearing this, a man can blunt the best sword and strew the ground with corpses."

The King beamed his pleasure at my sincere praise.

"We have a hundred of these coats, brought from Normandy. Alas, I cannot fit all my men with them. You will be needing this coat all too soon, my friend. Practise your battle moves. See that its weight becomes easy to bear."

"Are you planning a fight, Lord?"

The King pointed down the long fjord, "That way lies Steinker, a merchant town. Jarl Svein Hakonarson tied up his long-ship there and is preparing for the Yule feast. He will not give up without a struggle the lands the Swedes seized after defeating Olaf Trygvason at the battle of Svolder. That is why he has sailed up the coast from your part of the world, Ulf. My spies inform me he has met with his wife-brother, Einar, and means to assemble men to defeat me. But, as a descendant of Harald Fairhair, I am the true King of Norway. We will feed him to the ravenous fowl, Ulf. At all costs, we must not allow him to escape. We have him trapped in the fjord."

This reasoning was sound but Svein, a wily character, ordered his movable goods and meat and drink stowed aboard his ship. He rowed out at night-time until at daybreak he came to Skarnsund. From this position, he spied our ships in the fjord and turned his vessel towards the land within Masarvik where a thick wood grew. He steered his craft so near the rocks that the leaves and branches hung over the vessel. He ordered his men to cut down trees and laid them over the deck on the sea-side so that the ship could not be seen for leaves. We must have passed and failed to observe them when the light was poor. Taking advantage of the calm weather, our fleet rowed in among the islands. The sly fox waited in his den until our vessels were out of sight and fled to Frosta, where his kingdom lay, and where he landed.

There, Einar counselled caution to Svein, advising him to let

King Olaf know that they were not raising men but keeping quiet. In this way, the King would remain at Steinker over Yule, where everything was made ready for the feasting. Einar warned that if Olaf learnt they were gathering men, he would depart the fjord forthwith and then they would not be able to lay hold of him. We later discovered this plan, which lured us to Steinker. There, Olaf collected all the meat and drink prepared for the Yule feast, loaded it on transport vessels and sailed out to Nidaros.

Here King Olaf Trygvason once laid out a merchant town where he included the building of a king's house. Now, dilapidated from neglect, when we inspected the buildings they proved barely habitable.

"What do you think, Ulf? Can it be done by Yuletide?"

"We have many men to toil on it, my Lord."

Olaf decided to set our men to work, repairing the repairable and building anew those houses that had fallen down. On completion, our men brought ashore the meat and drink and I enjoyed a memorable feast after Bishop Grimkel and other priests conducted my first Christ's Mass.

The news coming in from our envoys was less than comforting. Although our religion spread hope and goodwill with the birth of our Saviour, war hung heavy in the air. Taxes due lay at the heart of the dispute. Svein had, as was custom, taken a half of the harbour-dues from the Icelandic traders coming to the Throndhjem country. The men King Olaf sent to demand the dues were driven away, fobbed off with a few skins.

Svein and Einar Tambaskelfer gathered a force of two thousand men and moved with stealth along the upper road to Gaulardal to drop down and fall upon Nidaros. As a wise precaution, Olaf had placed a guard with horses on the Gaular ridge. They spotted the foe and risked their necks by galloping to bring word to us near midnight. King Olaf ordered the people to wake and board the ships, bearing clothes and arms and all else they could take with them. Our fleet rowed out of the River Nid. Visible from the fjord, the red flare of firelight against the blackness of the night bespoke of the fate of the new town, burnt to the ground by Jarl Svein's army.

King Olaf's face was drawn and pale.

"Svein will pay for this, Ulf," he said through gritted teeth.

"Where shall we go, Lord?"

I half hoped to convince him to sail down to Trøndelag so I could embrace my Estrid. Indeed, we sailed out of the fjord and down the coast, but only as far as Orkadal where we landed. Whatever plan the King had was not clear at first. He marched us from Orkadal over the mountains eastwards into Gudbrandsdal. Thence, we headed down to Hedemark. The winter, as harsh thereabouts as ever, he countered by moving from one guest-quarters to another. With the welcome arrival of spring, we collected men from the powerful lesser kings on the way to Viken. This task was smoothed by Olaf's step-father, Sigurd Syr, who successfully petitioned his peers so that I was amazed at the great body of men we gathered. With this army, we marched to the coast and made ready to put to sea from Viken.

Informants arrived with news of Svein, who had not been idle. Proclaiming a levy of men from the Throndhjem country, he fitted out ships. Owing to his friendship with the leading *lendermen*, and his alliance with Einar, his numbers were formidable. They included some *lendermen* and *bondes* who had taken the oath of fidelity to Olaf. When they were ready, they sailed south and our informants told of how they gathered men from every district on their way. Thence, they steered eastwards, their fleet like a vast floating island on the sea, towards Viken which they approached as Easter drew nigh. The jarl chose to run his vessels into Nesjar.

Well aware of the approaching enemy, King Olaf took his ships out of Viken and sighted the foe on the Saturday before Palm Sunday. The next morning, he had the army land to hear his address.

"Now, we shall make ready, for it can be but a short time until we meet. Arm yourselves, be at the post to which you are appointed, so you will be ready when I order the signal sounded for casting off from the land."

King Olaf cut a fine figure as he spoke, and I admired the measured and confident tone of his words. Like every man assembled there, I was prepared to follow him even unto the maws of Hell. The King gazed around us, holding every man in thrall. He raised a finger to indicate the importance of his next speech.

"At the signal, let us row off at once; and so that none go on before the rest of the ships, and none lag behind when I leave the harbour. We cannot tell whether we shall find the enemy fleet where it was lying, or whether he will come out to meet us. When we engage them, and the battle begins, be alert to bring all our ships in close order, ready to bind together." He waved his finger around us. "At the beginning, take care of our weapons. Do not cast them into the sea or shoot them into the air to no purpose. Be calm. When the fight becomes hot and the ships are bound together, then let each man show what he possesses of manly spirit."

"Ay!" roared a hundred voices amid more general cheering.

The King raised his hand and my ears strained to catch his words.

"Remember your prayers, brothers, for God is with us. This day we shall drive the foreign upstart out of our land."

I too was a Swede, but at that moment felt I belonged with my Norse comrades. I had not fought since campaigning in England and was now ready for battle.

Like the other hundred men on our ship, I pulled on my coat of ring-mail and the unfamiliar helmet with its pale-coloured cross painted in front. My shield also bore a red painted cross, while others were emblazoned in blue. The King stood under his white banner, which figured a serpent, and stared around in satisfaction. He ordered a mass to be read and afterwards food and drink to be shared out.

At last, the order came for the war-horns to sound to battle, to leave the harbour, to seek the foe. Rowing towards the place where the enemy fleet had lain, we found the jarl's men armed. When they saw us drawing near they began to bind their ships together and to set up their banners. King Olaf urged our oarsmen to greater effort, laying our ship alongside Svein's, and the battle of Nesjar commenced.

They grappled and lashed our vessel so that sword on sword they boarded us, but steel-clad we pressed them hard. They had more men but the King had a chosen crew that had followed him in all his wars. Our coats of ring-mail meant we could not be wounded and the limb-lopping was in our favour. Our serpent banner, carried across the blood-slicked deck, reached the enemy ship and King Olaf himself followed the banner with me at his side. We pressed into the severest fighting where many of Svein's men fell, and some sprang overboard. The jarl saw how the fighting turned against him, called to the men in the prow to cut the cables and cast his vessel loose. Our men threw grapplings over the timber heads of the enemy craft, so holding her fast to our own, but Svein ordered the timber heads to be cut away. They sprang back onto their own vessel and our prize escaped, for Einar had lain his ship alongside the Jarl's. His crew cast an anchor over the bows of the enemy ship and towed her away. Thus, to our frustration, they slipped out of the fjord together. Thereafter the whole of the defeated fleet took to flight, though their losses were grave.

We followed them out to sea and noted that Svein had gathered his ships together. The King's step-father urged him: "King Olaf, make haste, let steel decide our cause!"

"Let us first watch for what the Jarl means to do; keep his force together or discharge the fleet."

"It is for you, King, to command," replied Sigurd Syr. "But, I fear, from your disposition and wilfulness, that you will someday be betrayed by trusting those people, for they are accustomed of old to bid defiance to their sovereigns."

We turned back because soon it was clear the enemy fleet was dispersing. Our ships hooked and hauled aboard many a floating corpse to ransack the slain and divide the booty. Later, King Olaf gave his step-father and the other chiefs who had assisted him some handsome presents. I received a war-horn of walrus-tusk ivory, carved and bound in beaten wrought gold.

"Sound the horn of victory!" Olaf commanded me and thumped me on my back so hard when I had done so that I was glad of my ring-mail coat.

"We will send out spies, Ulf, to trace Svein's doings."

Not until they returned and he found he had left the country, did we, the victors, sail out west to Viken. There, many people came to him and he was proclaimed King. Without proceeding further, we sailed with a steady wind to the Throndhjem country.

"In Throndhjem is the greatest strength of the land, Ulf, and no man shall contest me in Norway if I subdue it for myself while Svein is abroad."

How wise this decision proved. When King Olaf came to Throndhjem he met with no opposition and was elected King. At harvest time, he took his seat in the town of Nidaros, which he had rebuilt and where he collected the winter provision. One of his first enterprises was to construct the church of Clement. The ground he parcelled out, giving it to *bondes*, merchants and warriors to build upon. King Olaf did not trust the men of the interior of the district and he showed this by erecting defences in case Svein should return to the country.

This threat soon gained confirmation from a spy in the court of Svithjod, where his wife-brother, the Swedish King, promised him men to conquer the country again from Olaf. They resolved to take the land-way over Helsingjaland and Jamtaland in the winter, thus bringing them down into Throndhjem. The Jarl reckoned upon the faithful help and strength of the inland Throndhjem people as soon as he should arrive among them.

Meanwhile, Svein decided to sail around the Baltic in the summer months to raid and plunder. Jarl Svein marauded into Russia but as the autumn approached he returned to Svithjod. He became sick, and after a short time his soul departed this Earth.

12

NIDAROS 1016-1017 AD

The reconstructed Nidaros, arisen anew like a phoenix from the ashes, provided us with comfortable winter quarters. Snug we may have been but under no illusions that peace might endure or be enjoyed. The festering hatred and resentment of the King of Sweden reached a pitch where his own courtiers dared not nominate King Olaf within his hearing.

The arrival in Svithjod of Einar Tambaskelfer at the court of the King of Sweden exacerbated his mood. On learning from him how King Olaf had settled on his tributary lands, he determined to act. Einar informed him that after the death of Svein, the population of Throndhjem preferred Olaf. The latter, he said, had gone to every district in the autumn, holding meetings known as Things, taking oaths of allegiance and revenue.

The King's Hall in Nidaros had a door at each end with his throne in the centre. Arranged next to and around it, in the most honoured positions, were seats for Bishop Grimkel and his priests. Outside them sat the King's trusted counsellors and beyond them sixty courtiers and thirty chosen followers. To wait upon them, thirty house servants were aided by numerous slaves. Near to the hall stood outbuildings where the courtiers slept. I liked Nidaros and would willingly have established home there had it not been for my yearning for Estrid's warm embrace. This longing grew as the months advanced and King Olaf showed no sign of releasing me from my service. Understandable as this was, given the conflicting ambitions of the Kings of Norway and of Sweden, I chafed at my homely confinement.

In the winter of that year, the King of Sweden sent messengers over the mountain ridge to Veradal. Their first act, the summoning of a Thing of the *bondes,* led to a haughty demand for taxes. The local leaders, faced by a double levy, replied that they would pay only if King Olaf of Norway did not claim the same tax. With reason they refused to settle both. The emissaries proceeded down the valley with their retinue of twenty-four warriors but at every Thing they obtained only the same answer and no money. Worse followed at Stjoradal, where the *bondes* had the temerity not to attend the Thing. Realising their mission was failing, the envoys decided to come to Nidaros to present their case.

King Olaf received the messengers, two brothers, Thorgaut and Asgaut, in his Thing-house. Thorgaut spoke, and I admired his courage, telling our King first what his errand was and next how the Throndhjem folk had replied to it. With due deference but no servility, Thorgaut asked the King's decision on the business that they might know what result their mission was to achieve.

I tensed, having seen Olaf fly into a rage at much less provocation. But the King answered in a measured tone.

"While the jarls, who were of the royal race of the kingdom, ruled over the country, it was not to be wondered at if the people believed themselves bound to obey. It would have been just had these jarls given assistance and service to the kings who had a right to the country, rather than to foreign kings. Or to stir up opposition to their lawful kings..." and here it became clear to me that Olaf's fury was mounting and I feared for the safety of the brothers. My belief is that messengers are never to be held to blame under any circumstances.

Olaf finished, "...depriving them of their land and territory. With regard to the Swede who calls himself entitled to the kingdom of Norway, I, who in fact am so designated, can see no grounds for his claim. On the other hand, I well remember the damage we have suffered from him and his relations."

Thorgaut paled, looked perplexed and stood as if weighing his next words but Asgaut had no such hesitation and I marvelled at his audacity. "Your haughty reply, Lord, is ill-judged, for you cannot see how heavy our King's wrath will be for you to support, as many have experienced who had greater strength than you appear to have..."

When would the explosion come? My nails dug into the palm of my hand. "...but if you wish to retain your kingdom, it will be best for you to come to the King, and be his man; and we shall beg him to give you this land in fief under him."

I stood mouth open in amazement as King Olaf replied with unexpected gentleness, "I will give you advice, Asgaut, in exchange for yours. Go back to Svithjod to your King, and tell him that in early spring I will make myself ready, and will proceed eastwards to the ancient frontier that formerly divided our lands. There he may come if he chooses, that we may conclude peace and each will control the kingdom to which he is born."

The brothers went back to their lodgings and prepared for departure and the King went to table. That seemed to be the end of the matter until the spring – but not so. Later, we learned that Thorgaut and his brother were in disaccord. The former decided to return home with his men but Asgaut went into Gaulardal and Orkadal and meant to proceed to More to deliver his request for tribute. Word of this came to Olaf, who sent out a band of warriors to deal with them.

When their leader returned to Nidaros, I was in the hall and heard his account.

"Sire, we found them at the ness in Stein, bound their hands behind their backs, thence we led them to the point called Gaularas, where we raised a gallows..." Olaf leant forward, his eyes bright with interest, "...and hanged them so that they could be seen by anyone travelling the usual sea-way out of the fjord."

The King thumped on the table with his fist.

"By God, you did well. I should have slain the dogs here in this hall when they had the effrontery to address me with such disdain."

Thorgaut heard the news of his brother's doom before he travelled far on his way home. I can only imagine with what rage the King of Sweden received the tale of how it had gone with them.

After these events how could I broach my desire to return home? There was no chance of the peaceful outcome Olaf had mooted. The ferocious nature of the Swedes was matched only by that of the Norsemen. There was also the complication of the Danes. As a virtual outsider I had no grasp of the political situation, exactly as Estrid had accused me. To remedy this, I sought out one of the older *bondes*, a pleasant fellow named Brynjolf.

"Tell me, what is the root of the quarrel between the Swedes and the Norsemen? And what are the present circumstances?"

The greybeard sighed and feigned patience he cannot have felt.

"We *bondes* know where the division-boundaries between the Norwegian and Danish and Swedish kings' lands stood by rights in olden times. Do you know the Gaut river, Ulf?"

I nodded.

"It divided their lands between the Vener lake and the sea, thence towards the north, woodland marked the division up to the Eid forest. Thereafter, the ridge was the boundary all the way to the distant Finmark."

"Why is this no longer the case?"

One-eyed Brynjolf peered at me with his sound eye as if at an imbecile. He shook his head and said, "By turns they have made inroads upon each other's territories, and the Swedes have long had power all the way to Svinasund." He raised and wagged a finger as if to stress his point.

"In truth, I know many would rather serve the King of Norway, but they dare not. I include myself in that number, Ulf, for the King of Sweden's lands surround me, eastward, southward and also up the country. As things stand, King Olaf will soon go to the north, where the strength of his kingdom lies, and then I will have no power to withstand the Gautlanders. You see, Ulf, it is for Olaf to give us good counsel, for we have strong desire to be his men. Is that clearer now?"

Indeed, it was. Deeper gloom descended on me. Would I ever see my home again? I could smell war in the air.

In the following days, matters worsened because Brynjolf took every occasion to speak alone with Olaf and I felt certain it would lead to no good. My suspicions proved well-founded when Olaf came to me.

"Ulf, you will wear your ring-mail coat well concealed by a cloak and a hat over your helm. Likewise Brynjolf, Thorer Lange and six other men. You will follow me, dressed this way, aboard ship. Brynjolf knows what to do. Obey his orders."

My heart sank. A man does not disguise his intent unless he means ill. I could not defy my King so it was done. Olaf laid his ships close to a rocky knoll protruding into the sea. Upon the land, the King led us to a spot where he sat on a rock. Below was a flat field where Eilif of Gautland stood with men lined up in a shield wall.

An open battle is fair enough but to dress in disguise and pretend a parley is a villainous, cowardly act. Lured to the deliberations, Eilif listened to Bjorn the Marshal, who spoke long and cleverly on the King's account. In truth, I remember nought of his discourse because I waited, tense and uneasy, for the treachery to which I was an unwilling party to be consumed.

When at last Bjorn sat down Eilif stood to speak, but at the same moment Thorer Lange rose, drew his hidden sword, and struck Eilif on the neck, decapitating him. The horrified Gautland men, fearing further betrayal, fled and Brynjolf called us in pursuit of them. We smote several but this morning's work was not to my taste.

Upon our return to the knoll, the King was addressing the *bondes* he had brought to the false Thing. The end of it was they submitted to the King, promising fidelity and eliciting from Olaf an oath to remain nearby until the discord between him and the Swedes was settled. The whole northern district came under Olaf's power and by summer his authority stretched as far eastward as the Gaut river. He was also able to raise taxes among the islands.

As the summer drew to an end, he returned north to Viken and sailed up the river Raum to a waterfall named Sarp. On the far side of the fall, a point of land juts out into the river. Olaf ordered a rampart to be built across the ness. We dragged stone, cut turf and hewed wood to make the bulwark and dug a ditch in front of it. This large earthen fortress protected a burgh and Olaf made of it a merchant town. We constructed a King's house and erected a church dedicated to Mary, mother of the Lord. He drew plans for other houses and commanded people to build them. When harvest time arrived, he ordered everything to be gathered and brought sufficient for winter residence.

Neither he, nor any of us, expected peace after the murder of Eilif and to drive home his rancour, Olaf prohibited all exports of herrings and salt from Viken to Gautland. This was a grave blow to the folk of those lands. The King made plans for a great Yule feast, to which he decided to invite many of the foremost *bondes*.

This was my moment as 1017 approached. I had served the King for more than two years since his summons.

"Lord, I am ever faithful to you," I began, "but the time has come for me to return to my wife and lands until such time as you need me."

King Olaf stared hard at me from under his sandy golden eyebrows and his blue eyes held a warmth the likes of which I had not dared to hope for.

"Ulf, you are a true friend and I will sorely miss you at Yuletide but you have the right of it. I have kept you apart from your family long enough. Go with my blessing. But I beseech you to come with your men when the need arises – as it surely will."

My oath sworn, I sailed with the Trøndelag crew who had stayed with me throughout these years of exile. My men, like me, were in good spirits to be returning home. Their exuberance increased by the lavish gifts Olaf thought to bestow on them. Not just coin did he provide for them but also food and drink for their families at Yuletide. To a man they were loyal to their Norse King but never so fond of him as at this time. Not one of us returned home without sadness at leaving our King and none of us were deluded as to the likelihood of peace. War, we knew, was in the offing.

13

TRØNDELAG, 1016-17 AD

One of the advantages of having a distinctive design on your sails is that folk with keen eyesight announce early your arrival to everyone. Thus when I leapt, eager to be home, onto the jetty, I found Estrid lurking like a lynx about to spring into my arms. Lithe and sensuous as a feline and as difficult to detach, she set about me with a hail of questions. They did not cease until I planted a kiss on her lips once through the doorway to our hall.

The hunger of her mouth matched mine and I began to grab at the fastenings of her dress.

"Come, husband, to the bedchamber," she tugged at my hand. But her strength was no match for my battle-hardened muscles and I hauled her into my arms, much as I might gather my shirt from the back of a chair. Lifting her off her feet, grabbing a cushion from a bench, I deposited her, laughing and protesting on it, in front of the fire. My feverish hands tugged at her clothing, drawing her dress above her waist.

"Ulf! Stop that at once! What if anyone were to come into the hall?"

My lips closed over hers. I had been so long away from my wife and her resisting made me want her more. Besides, I could sense her unwillingness was a sham. The reaction of her body as I entered her confirmed my supposition. Our firstborn was conceived there beside the fire and never was a child born of more love and passion.

As we lay panting next to each other, Estrid whispered, "Ulf, there is a wonderful surprise awaiting you."

"It cannot match what we have done here, my love."

"But I am sure it will please you greatly. He must have waited to give us time together, thank God!"

"He? Who?"

"What surprise would it be if I told you?" Her eyes sparkled with mischief.

"And yet you will tell," I said, tickling her without mercy.

But she did not and it was not until I was sitting quaffing ale at a table that a figure arrived, his face obscured by the light beyond the door.

"Ulf, well met!"

The voice, familiar to me since childhood, for once exuded warmth.

"Brother!" I cried, "Come drink with me!"

How strange! I was pleased to see Eilaf, our differences forgotten in my glow of pleasure at being home amongst family. The arduous campaigning with Olaf, the rigours of the terrain, fjords and combat faded into nothingness compared to my homecoming.

"When did you come, Eilaf?"

"Some days ago. I wanted to be the one to break the news."

"I am sure you have much to tell, for more than two years have passed since we last spoke."

"Indeed."

What ailed him? His face grew solemn and he studied mine.

"I am the bearer of ill tidings, brother. Our father is no longer with us. His soul is in paradise with the angels."

"Eilaf! Have you become Christian?"

To my shame, this shocked me more than the loss of my beloved father.

"Along with all Cnut's men and my lord himself. In England, we all took the faith and, Ulf, I'm glad of it. I'm a better man for it." His face clouded and in sorrowful tone he added, "I have a great weight on my conscience. I will tell you later."

"What happened to father?"

"He sailed on a campaign with Jarl Svein to the land of the Wends and there fell in battle."

"As he always wished. He will dine with Odin in Valhalla."

I don't know why I said it; partly to comfort myself but also to provoke Eilaf.

He certainly had changed. With a smile of equanimity and a gentle voice, he said, "Dear brother, I know from Estrid you have been baptised...and it gives me joy."

I called for a beaker and poured him an ale.

"So now you are Jarl of Upsal?"

"I am, but I fear I shall not have much time to dedicate to our family holdings."

"How so?"

"Cnut released me from service only for the winter. He remains in England and here's the thing, before next spring is out I know he will be crowned King of that land."

That made me sit up, "Are you sure? So tell me, what has happened since I left the army?"

"Ulf, it's a long tale of valorous deeds, of squalid treachery and of noble gestures. You know that King Harald was crowned at Candlemas in 1014 and the people of the Danelaw elected Cnut as King in England?"

"Of course, I was there then. It's what happened afterwards that interests me."

"When we came back to Denmark, you too, he went straight to Harald and suggested joint kingship. You had sailed off by then. This found no favour with his brother who offered him command of the forces for another invasion of England, on the condition he did not continue to press his claim."

Eilaf took a long draught of ale, smacked his lips and continued his tale.

"In the summer of 1015, Ulf, we set sail for England. You should have seen the fleet! Two hundred long-ships and an army of ten thousand men - all noble warriors, no slaves, no-one unwilling, men from Sweden and Norway too. Gold shone on the prows, silver flashed in the various-shaped vessels. Some of the figureheads were bulls, Ulf, with horns shining with gold. Who could gaze upon them without feeling fear? When we landed, the fighting was close and gory. I swear I don't remember ferocious hand-play such as in that year."

"I am surprised the weakling Aethelred put up so much resistance."

"That's the point! *He* did not. But his son Edmund, known as 'the Ironside', fought all the battles and he is a valiant warrior."

"But you beat him?"

"At times."

I admit, I raised an eyebrow at that and began to yearn for the conflict I had missed until I thought of our glorious victory at Nesjar. Still, fighting was more to be had in England – or was that an impression? After all, before long King Olaf might call me to battle once more against the Swedes.

"So, you arrived with a vast fleet. Where did you go and what did you do?" I thirsted for his account.

"We went to Sandwich first and regrouped after the crossing, thence straightaway sailed around Kent to Wessex to the mouth of a river known as the Frome. We harried across the counties of Dorset, Wiltshire and Somerset – a fair land."

"So it is."

"Wessex submitted to Cnut late in 1015. I spoke earlier of betrayal," Eilaf's mouth turned down in disdain. "I'm sure the surrender came also because the Ealdorman of Mercia, Eadric

Streona – may he rot in Hell – deserted Aethelred and brought us forty ships with their crews. Do you remember Thorkell the Tall?"

"How could I forget that traitor?"

"He did it again, Ulf! This time, he came back to us with all his mercenaries."

"The snake."

Eilaf poured us both another ale, so rapt was I at his tale that I forgot my duties as host.

"He is a mighty combatant, Ulf and I believe he had a reason for his defection."

"How so?"

"You will remember how Aethelred betrayed me? I was lucky to escape with my life. The real serpent is *he*. Once more, he launched a disloyal attack on Thorkell and his men. Although it was conducted in secrecy and by vile surprise, the ferocious resistance of the victims was such that more than half escaped with their lives. Among the fallen was Thorkell's brother Henning."

"I am sorry to hear of Henning's death. He was a noble warrior and brave leader of men."

"True. You see, Thorkell had the right of it; our forces are strengthened with him at our side and our enemies much weakened."

We laughed at this and touched our beakers together in relaxed brotherly friendship. This pleased me, so Estrid's surprise turned out to be a pleasant one.

"When the winter passed, what did you do?"

"In that season still, we crossed the Thames and harried into Warwickshire, but Edmund failed to muster men and his army disbanded. By mid-winter, we devastated eastern Mercia and headed northwards. Edmund went north to join Uhtred the Earl of Northumbria and they ravaged Staffordshire, Shropshire and Cheshire. I reckon they wished for vengeance on the estates of Eadric Streona."

"What did Cnut do?"

"Ulf, he has become a true leader. Taking advantage of Uhtred's absence, he occupied Northumbria, forcing Uhtred to leave Edmund, return home and submit to him."

"Why that expression, brother?" I saw his face had clouded, "Was it not well done?"

"It was but..."

Eilaf paused and played with his cup as though to gain time for thinking. I was not wrong when I imagined he cast an anxious glance at my wife.

"...it does not sit well with me. See, Cnut befriended a rival of Uhtred, a Northumbrian lord known as Thurbrand the Hold. He massacred Uhtred and his retinue and although my lord denies all knowledge of this matter, I do not believe it. I think he arranged the whole thing." Eilaf sighed, "In any case, Northumbria is ours. At this point the old greybeard Eirikr Hakonarson came to England with his Norsemen and Cnut put him in charge of Northumbria...A clever move."

These words he added as an afterthought, I'm convinced to mollify Estrid, Cnut's sister. She did not seem out of sorts when she rose and excused herself to leave us alone.

"Cnut had a large part of England under his control by the spring of this year. But London is still in Aethelred's hands."

"You do not know then, brother? Aethelred died in April and Edmund Ironside took the throne."

"Ah, Aethelred is dead – good riddance! Though, I worry it will make the English stronger."

"Fear not on that account, Ulf. We have them on their knees. Are you sure you have the patience to hear more?"

"By God, ay I do! I want to know why you think Cnut will become King of England."

"We returned south and divided our forces. Thorkell and I led a force to deal with Edmund, who broke out of London and made for Wessex while Cnut encircled the city. He constructed dykes on the northern and southern flanks of London and dug a channel across the river banks to cut off communications upriver. We fought Edmund in

Somerset and then later at Sherston in Wiltshire over two days. It was hard and neither side could claim victory–"

At this point Estrid reappeared, carrying a freshly baked loaf, hot from the oven in a folded cloth.

"You two have used so much strength in yarning, I thought I ought to bring you food so you can attack once more."

We both laughed, grateful to slice into the steaming bread while Estrid gave orders for cheese, cold salted meat and more ale to be brought.

"So what are you talking about now?" Estrid asked.

"About how we captured London and how Cnut will become King of England," Eilaf said.

"Instead of more urgent things like you finding a bride." Estrid grinned wickedly.

"I've no time for that, sister. I will have to return to your brother, Cnut, as soon as Yuletide is over and the sea permits."

"You can take a shield-maiden with you. We have some very pretty and strong-built maids in Trøndelag."

"Brother, you are of an age to wed."

I smiled at him but he gave me a sour glare.

"Cnut has promised me an important Earldom in England when he is King. I know not which one but you see, nothing must impede me from going to make my fortune. First things first. Anyway, I may make an advantageous marriage if I'm single."

"I'll wager you'll find plenty of English blooms when you are an earl in that land," Estrid teased.

Eilaf ignored her and took up his tale again. A good-looking fellow like him would have no trouble finding a wife, I thought as he resumed.

"The problem, brother, is not what Cnut can give me but the price my soul has to pay for it."

"How so?"

"It's a long tale but it must be calmly told."

14

TRØNDELAG, 1017 AD

In truth, I was by now weary of Eilaf's account but I felt compelled to hear him out. The semblance of fever in his eyes spoke eloquently of his distress although hitherto there was nought in his tale to explain what so dismayed him. He continued as before.

"Edmund is a valiant warrior. He drove Cnut from London and defeated him at Brentford. But he suffered heavy losses as our men are hardy. Hence, he went to Wessex to gather more warriors. And so, we brought London under siege once more. Cnut tired of the lack of progress and launched an assault on English forces in Kent. The traitorous Eadric Streona went over to King Edmund. In a rage, Cnut sailed across the Thames estuary to Essex, thence took his vessels up the River Orwell to ravage Mercia in an act of vengeance. Two months ago, in October, as we retired towards our ships, Edmund's army met us and fought a terrible battle at Assandun."

"Why, what is the matter, brother?" Estrid exclaimed and seized his hand as Eilaf's face took on the grimmest of expressions.

"In the struggle, Eadric Streona – the weasel, whose return to the English side had been, we suspect, a ruse – betrayed Edmund, withdrawing his forces. We won a crushing victory. Edmund fled and we pursued him into Gloucestershire and near the Forest. We fought again but Edmund had support from the Welsh, so the battle was indecisive. But hark!"

We listened eagerly, but Eilaf stuffed his mouth with bread and cheese so our patience was tested until he chewed and swallowed his food.

"We met with Edmund, wounded as he was, on an island to negotiate peace. We agreed that England north of the Thames would be ours, while the south and London, he would keep."

"But who holds London, retains power in the land," I objected.

"Indeed, but there was one final agreement. The reign of the entire realm would pass to Cnut upon Edmund's death."

"What?"

"A risky accord, would you not agree? Two days before I sailed here, on the last day of November to be exact, Edmund died. Heed me well, brother and sister, but keep this to yourselves. I believe Cnut was responsible for his murder, though no-one breathes that word and none accuses your brother, Estrid. Forgive me, maybe I speak out of turn but it seems so convenient."

"Might he not have passed away from his wound?" Estrid asked.

I laughed, "You are too good, wife. As matters stand, it looks like you will be the sister of the King of England."

"The West Saxons have accepted him as King," Eilaf said, "and it is as good as done."

"You must be there for his crowning, Eilaf, else he may give the earldom to another. But now, I have heard about your adventures. Pour us another ale, Estrid, and I will tell you both about mine."

"All in good time Ulf, but first you must hear what so burdens my soul. You have heeded me well. Have patience for I too have need of it." As he spoke, the hand holding his drinking vessel shook and I saw agitation consume him.

"Do you recall my mentioning the treacherous Eadric Streoner?"

"Ay – a serpent."

"It is of Eadric I must recount. How long is it since Christ's Mass?"

The question surprised me and I frowned, counting the days silently.

"It is less than a moon. Maybe thirteen days."

"It is so. A fortnight ago, King Cnut summoned me to a private audience. I could see he was ill at ease. 'Eilaf,' says he, 'you have ever been a loyal servant and now I have a boon to ask. We must pay what we owe to Eadric Streoner.' At first, I thought he was speaking of coin but I soon learnt the debt he referred to was one of vengeance..." Eilaf sighed and stared , head bowed over the table. When he resumed, his countenance was twisted as if in pain, "...'this Streoner,' says Cnut, 'is a viper. You ought to know he is from a humble family and has risen to wealth and high rank only by means of smooth-talking deception. He is capable of feigning anything. The man is rife with faults – a sinner, a glutton and a purloiner of Church lands and funds. But worse, Eilaf,' says the King and stares at me as if to bend me to his will, 'he is a fiend and betrayer of honour, a murderer. Much of what he's done was at the command of the slimy Aethelred. Do you know what his first crime was, Eilaf?' I confessed I did not."

" 'I will relate it.' I see now, Ulf, the King was stirring me to a deed." Eilaf sighed again and glowered at something over my shoulder so severely that I almost turned but realised he was scowling at his recollections. "... Cnut continued, 'At Aethelred's instigation, Streoner invited Elfhelm, the Ealdorman of York, to his residence in Shrewsbury but before so doing, beguiled the town butcher, Godwin Porthund. With jewels and promises of further riches he bought his malicious service. Is there a worse crime than betraying hospitality, Eilaf? After receiving Elfhelm as an intimate friend, the smooth-tongued devil took him hunting in the woods, where this Godwin sprang out and slew the unsuspecting ealdorman. This is only the first of many crimes the villain has perpetrated. Some weeks later, he ordered the blinding of Elfhelm's sons, Wulfheah and Ufegeat, for fear of what they otherwise might do.' "

"By now, Ulf, it was clear to me what Cnut wanted of me. I protested, but in a timid way, that I was no murderer but his mind was set. What was I to do? I was in no position to disobey my liege. You *do* understand, do you not, Ulf?"

It seemed my comprehension mattered to him, so I reached across the table and took his hand. I thought of father's words to me long ago: *'Moral courage, Ulf, is not something that blows in the wind or changes with the weather. It is within a man. It is the decisive factor determining character. Looking inside yourself and drawing upon it, means you will ever do what is right. The doing is more important than the knowing'* I strove to form some comforting words for Eilaf based on that same advice but the delay cost me and he spoke first.

"Oh, the irony of it, Ulf! The King condemned Eadric Streoner for breaking the custom of hospitality but then plotted to do the same. This was the eve of Christ's Mass – a sacred, holy time. 'Eilaf,' says Cnut, 'tomorrow, there will be great feasting to celebrate the birth of our Saviour, and what better time than when a man is in his cups? Slay him and his friends. Choose three trusted companions. Claim insult – any excuse to do the deed. Serve me well in this and I will show you what it means to please your sovereign.' So there you have it, Ulf, plainer than that–"

"The festivity began after Mass in mid-afternoon and a long evening stretched before us. I planned everything to the last detail. I bought one of Streoner's servants for a considerable bag of silver. His task was to lure his master outdoors with a concocted story to Eadric's advantage. We four assailants hid our weapons near the agreed location. Another servant I paid to ply Streoner with drink throughout the evening, a duty he carried out to perfection. When we saw Streoner's man in my pay whisper in his ear, it was our signal to rise and leave the hall as unobtrusively as we could."

"Eadric Streoner came staggering towards us, the worse for strong ale. Ulf, will I ever find peace again?"

The anguish on his face struck me as peculiar. Here was a warrior, hardened in battle and no stranger to slaughter, suffering for having dispatched a treacherous murderer. As I saw it, I decided he had rid the world of the worst of scoundrels. I did not hesitate to tell him so, but my words had little effect.

"You do not understand, Ulf. The plotting to lure him to his doom was not a manly deed. In his cups and defenceless, it would have been no harder to slay an infant. I shall never forget the hatred and horror in his eyes as I raised my axe to strike his head from his body. At least his end was mercifully swift."

"But you pleased your King. Is that not comfort enough?"

"We compounded the crime by slaying his friends who came from the hall to seek him. Cnut wanted them dead too – noblemen – Northman, son of Leofwine, Aethelweard, son of Aethelmaer the Stout and Brithic, the son of the Ealdorman of Devon. They were unarmed as weapons are not permitted at the King's feast. Ulf, they stood no chance – on one of the holiest days of the year. Does not the Commandment tell us not to kill?"

"Indeed, but killing is our duty as warriors of God's anointed King. Set your mind at rest, brother. Or do you intend to become a monk and live out your life in penitence?"

His face lit up for a moment and he forced a bitter laugh at the absurdity of such an idea but the lightening of his countenance was momentary. His visage twisted again into a grimace.

"You haven't heard the worst of it, Ulf. Do you know what Cnut did?"

I shook my head.

"He ordered Eadric's head to be impaled on a stake on the highest battlement and his body to be flung over the town walls, to be left unburied."

"A fitting end for a traitor. What are your qualms?"

"Ulf! I slew him at Christ's Mass and he did not obtain a Christian burial. I doomed him to Hell, where I will surely join him."

Impressed as I was by my brother's religious fervour – a side to his character I never dreamt of seeing – I could find no words to comfort him.

"Worse still–"

"There is worse?"

"Ay. I was compelled to slay the servant I had bought to betray his master. We could not risk loose talk. Had we been denounced as the murderers, King Cnut would have had an awkward predicament. So I slit his throat in his bed that night and reclaimed the bag of silver. O; I am doomed for all eternity!"

The time had come to distract Eilaf from his self-flagellation and to do so, I recounted all the events I had endured in his absence.

The telling took a full hour but at the end I was gratified to see him relaxed and interested. I declared, "You see Eilaf, our paths must separate – you'll go your way and I'll go mine. Let us enjoy what's left of this Yuletide together, for who knows when we'll meet again?"

I stood and embraced him, glad to have made peace with my brother. Would I have been so contented had I been able to foresee the future? Are we not all the sum of what our fathers make us for better or for worse?

15

TRØNDELAG, 1017-1018 AD

Only after Christ's Mass and Eilaf's departure did I consider that as Swedes we were both serving foreign monarchs. He was returning to Cnut, a Dane, and I served Olaf, a Norseman. This led to the shocking thought that if war did come with Sweden, I would be fighting my own people again. Father had died following Svein. If he had not, in war I might have found myself facing my own parent in battle. I shuddered at the concept and only the thought that Eilaf was far away in England soothed me. It made me more determined to take up the cause of peace so yearned for by the Gautlanders.

The alarming news of one crisis after another and the resulting air of strife in the winter of 1017 drove me to abandon the loving comfort of Estrid's embraces. Duty called me to seek out Olaf. The decisive moment that spurred my decision was the arrival in our harbour of a Viking cutter commanded by Eyvind Urarhorn.

A man of high birth, Eyvind went out on a Viking cruise every summer, sometimes in the West sea, other times in the Baltic. Also, he had fought beside us at Nesjar. While dining, he told me Olaf had sent for him, and thereafter at his behest he sailed south towards

Viken. In the area of Eikreys Isle, he learned that Hroe Skialge had gone northwards to Ordost to make a levy of men and goods on account of the Swedish King. His ship was expected at any moment from the north. Bent on intercepting him, Eyvind rowed in by Haugasund. There he met Hroe and fought, killing him and his thirty men and taking all his wares before proceeding on yet another Viking cruise.

Eyvind next asked me whether I knew about a great merchant called Gudleik Gerske.

"No? I can tell you, Lord Ulf, he travels far and wide by sea and is very rich. He often goes east to Russia, hence his name which means 'the Russian'. That is where he intended to go this spring after fitting out his ship. Olaf sent a message saying he wanted to speak to him, then asked him to buy costly items, hard to find here in Norway, providing the necessary money. So, Gudleik set out for the Baltic.

"They lay in a sound in Gotland... and you know, Ulf..." his green eyes bored into mine, and a smile more like a sneer curled his lip, "...how people cannot keep their secrets. Soon, everyone knew the ship was Olaf's partner. Gudleik went in the summer to Novgorod, where he bought fine and expensive clothes, intended for Olaf as state dress, as well as furs and valuable utensils. In autumn on the way back to Norway, he met contrary winds and lay for a long time in the lee of the island of Eyland. There came Thorgaut Skarde, who knew of Gudleik's course—"

"Sup another ale! Let me guess. He gave him battle?"

"He did!"

Eyvind stretched out his beaker for my servant to fill. Heaven knows with such a long tale to tell, another drink would not go amiss. A swift draught and he took up his account.

"They fought long, and Gudleik and his men defended bravely, but overcome, Gudleik and many of his crew fell and many were wounded. Thorgaut took all their goods which they divided among themselves, and Olaf's, which they decided should go to the King of Sweden. This, they said was only fair—"

"How so?"

"As compensation for the taxes due from Norway taken by Hroe Skialge."

"So, he took the goods to Olof the Swede, did he?"

"Hold! For my tale is not ended. He headed east for Svithjod with that intent. By chance, I arrived soon after he left at Eyland and discovered the news. How tongues will wag! I overtook them among the Swedish isles off the coast and attacked."

"Well done, Eyvind!"

I raised my beaker to him and grinned. I liked this fellow.

"We slew Thorgaut and most of his men. The rest sprang overboard. We took back the goods they had seized and all the costly articles meant for the sovereign. Then we burnt their long-ship. Now I am on my way to Olaf with his precious wares."

"He will be well pleased to receive them. Shame about Gudleik."

"Ay."

I stared at Eyvind. "Hark, I also was planning to depart at once, for I must go to Olaf."

"Come with me, friend, and welcome."

"Right gladly. We can leave at dawn."

We landed at Viken, for our ruler had gone into Gautland and would have followed him, carts laden with goods, as far as the Gaut river. Olaf met there with Jarl Ragnvald to consider the loss caused to the Gautlanders and the people of Viken by the bad blood between the overlords of Norway and Sweden. There was no peace for trade. By returning to Viken before we set off, Olaf saved us the journey.

He was delighted with Eyvind and to see me. But the joy of receiving his gifts was tempered by the mood among the *bondes* of Viken. Nobody dared broach the subject of their murmurings to the monarch, but they begged Bjorn the marshal to bring the matter of their hardships occasioned by the kings at war. They entreated him to send messengers to Olof Eirikson to offer peace on his side. Reluctant to do this, Bjorn came to me to discuss his worries because he knew Olaf would take it ill to give any concessions to the Swedish King.

As luck turned out, Hjalte Skeggjason arrived from Iceland and was well received by the monarch in good fellowship.

"Bjorn," I said, "this is heaven-sent. Hjalte is the man we need. Tell him of the situation and implore his aid."

"How can he help me, Ulf?"

"He is neutral in this matter, well-respected for his sagacity, and also our sovereign holds him in high esteem. He is well-placed to raise the issue. Take him into your confidence."

Bjorn did so and Olaf agreed to consider his arguments after Hjalte's intervention. These are the words of Bjorn:

"What think you, Lord, of the strife that is between Olof Eirikson and you? Many people have fallen on both sides, without it being at all more determined than before what each of you shall take of the kingdom. You have now sat for one winter and two summers in Viken, and the whole country to the north is lying behind your back unseen. The men with property or rights in the north are weary of sitting here. It is the wish of the *lendermen*, of your other people, and of the *bondes* that this should come to an end. There is now peace with Jarl Ragnvald and the Gautlanders. It appears to the people best if you send messengers to the Swedish ruler to offer a reconciliation on your side. Without doubt many who are about Olof will support the proposal, for it is a common gain for those who dwell in both countries, here and there."

This speech received crashing applause. For but a moment Bjorn was gratified, but the monarch soon removed the smile from his countenance.

"It is only fair, Bjorn, that the advice you have given should be carried out by yourself. You will undertake the embassy and reap the benefits of it."

The next day I met with Bjorn and asked, "Why are you so gloomy? Are you sick or angry at anyone?"

He made reference to his conversation with Olaf and ended, "It is a very dangerous errand, Ulf."

"It is the lot of great men who enjoy high honours and respect to stand often in danger. You must understand how to bear both parts of your destiny. Much renown will be gained from this business if it succeeds."

"Since you make so light of it, Ulf, will you come with me? Our sovereign says I may take companions."

"On one sole condition - that Hjalte Skeggjason accompanies us."

Bjorn met with Hjalte and persuaded him to come with us. Successful in this, he went to Olaf to receive instructions and his farewells.

"Carry these my words to the Swedish overlord– I will establish peace between our countries up to the frontier which Olaf Trygvason had before me. Each shall bind himself faithfully not to trespass over it. No further mention as to the loss of people must be made, for Olof Eirikson cannot with money pay for the men they deprived us of."

Thereupon Olaf rose and went with Bjorn to join his followers, a dozen of us, where he handed him a gold-mounted sword and a gold ring.

"I give you these, received from Jarl Ragnvald this summer. Give him the ring, a token he will know, and ask him to advance your errand with his counsel and strength."

A warm welcome awaited us at Jarl Ragnvald's court but when Bjorn presented the gold band and explained his mission, the Jarl gazed around us with a grave expression.

"What have you done, Bjorn, that the King wishes your death? Where can a man be found to utter these words to Olof Eirikson without incurring his wrath and punishment? He is too proud to listen to what angers him."

At this point, I intervened, "Forgive me Lord, but should it be said the message of King Olaf was neglected from fear of the Swede? You possess birth, strength of relations, and other means, so that you can speak your mind and sway the people in our favour."

"You tell the truth, Lord Ulf. I shall aid you so you may lay your errand before Olof, whether he take it ill or well. But you will all follow my advice for this is not a matter to be entered into with haste."

We remained for some weeks at the Jarl's court but Bjorn grew uneasy at the long delay. Tired of the marshal's exasperation, Hjalte said, "I will go to this monarch, for I am not a man of Norway, and the Swedes hold nothing against me. I believe there are Icelanders in the royal household who are my acquaintances: the skalds Gissur and Ottar Black. From them I will learn much about Olof Eirikson. I must have Ulf with me for he is a Swede and ever gives me sound counsel." It was thus agreed and going to the Jarl's wife, Ingebjorg, we told her of our plans. She gave us silver coins and two Gautlander guides and tokens to present to the King's daughter, Ingegerd, to enlist her aid in Hjalte's business.

We set off at once and when we came to the Swedish court, Hjalte soon found the skalds who were glad at his coming. Without delay they went to the sovereign to tell him about the arrival of their countryman – one of the most considerable in their native land. Since the skalds were often in the royal household, Hjalte became known to the monarch, who willingly heard news of Iceland. Soon they enjoyed good fellowship. The Icelander bided his time until one night, Olof was very merry and drunk. I was sitting close enough to hear their conversation and Hjalte spoke thus:

"Much splendour and grandeur have I seen here. I can state without fear of contradiction no monarch in the north is so magnificent. But it is most vexatious that we who come so far to visit you endure a road so long and troublesome. It is not safe to travel through Norway for those who wish to come here in friendship. Why does no-one bring proposals of peace between you and Olaf the Thick? Much is spoken in Norway and in Gautland of the general desire that this reconciliation should take place. Olaf, it is said, earnestly desires it. I know this is so because he recognises how much less is his power than yours. I believe he wishes to pay court to your daughter Ingegerd, which would lead to a useful peace."

I bit my lip and lowered my head for I did not wish it to be seen that I was taking too close an interest in this discussion. At this crucial moment, I feared the monarch's reaction. In fact, his stare at Hjalte was icy and his words as cold.

"For this time, I will not take it amiss of you, Hjalte, for you do not know what people must avoid here. That fat fellow must not be called King in my court. Such a connection is unsuitable, for I am the tenth king in Upsal, who has been sole monarch over Sweden and other great lands. All were superior over others in the northern countries. But Norway is little inhabited, and the people are scattered. Only small rulers live there. Even the greatest, Harald Harfanger, who subdued the small kings, did not dare covet Swedish possessions. When Olaf Trygvason came to Norway and proclaimed himself King, we could not permit it. We went with Sweyn Forkbeard and cut him off. Thus we appropriated Norway and conquered the monarchs who ruled before. Hjalte, you will not speak on this subject again in my presence."

There and then, I decided our only hope was an approach to Ingegerd. The next day, I went to her and presented the tokens sent by Ingebjorg. I begged her to say a good word to her father, but she replied, "Speak about it I will, but he will listen as little to me as to Hjalte."

I trailed her into the royal hall and remained in the shadows near a wall, close enough to follow her plea.

"Father, there are many who complain about your wars with Olaf of Norway, having lost their property by it. Others have seen their relations dispatched by the Norsemen and all their peace and quiet. It would be bad counsel if you sought dominion over Norway. It is a poor country, difficult to come at and the people hardy warriors who would serve any other monarch but you. Let go all designs on Norway but rather turn your thoughts to the east. Your forefathers held those lands. Reclaim them but first, make peace with Olaf."

At these last words, the sovereign who had listened patiently to his daughter flew into a rage.

"Never!" he roared, "Is it your counsel, Ingegerd, that I should let slip the kingdom of Norway? No, rather than that, at the Upsal Thing in winter, I will issue a proclamation to all Swedes that the people shall assemble for an expedition. They will go to their ships before the ice is off the waters. We will proceed to Norway and lay waste to the land with fire and sword, and burn everything to punish them for their want of fidelity."

Her father was so mad with rage that Ingegerd retreated without another word. I followed her and begged her to hear me once more.

"May I be permitted, daughter of the King, to tell you what lies on my mind?"

"Speak freely, Lord Ulf, but for my ears alone."

"What would be your answer if Olaf were to send messengers to you with the errand to propose marriage?"

She blushed and said, "I made no decision on that, but if Olaf is as perfect as you tell me, I would wish for no other husband. Unless, Lord Ulf, you have gilded his qualities with your praise."

I assured her I had not and we often spoke in private on the same subject. Ingegerd begged me to be discreet and not mention it to anyone. I did not, but by happy chance Hjalte also addressed her regarding Olaf's virtues. I sent the two Gautlanders back to the Jarl's wife, Ingebjorg, with a message about this possible plan.

In truth, I felt peace with Sweden hung by this slender thread and did not hold out much hope of success. Bear in mind that as a seer, I had not the slightest reputation.

16

RINGSAKER, 1017 AD

In Norway and England other important events were taking place, which I was informed of later. Here is what happened. Olaf decided to transfer to guest lodgings in the Uplands. Custom required the Norse kings to visit the area every third year and Olaf wished to uphold this usage. When he arrived, however, to his disgust he found a deep-rooted tradition of paganism. As a deeply devout Christian, he determined to root it out by any means. His methods included mutilation, killing or exile and this created much resentment and ferment among the population and its five kings.

They met together by the lake at Ringsaker to discuss their fears and what to do, since Olaf was nearby with almost four hundred men. Two options faced them: submit to Olaf and lose their traditions or raise an army between them and overcome his forces, not a number too vast for them to meet.

King Gudrod spoke thus: "We are here five kings and none of less high birth than Olaf. We gave him the strength to fight Jarl Svein and with our men, he has brought the country under his power. But if he grudges us our traditions in the little kingdoms we hold and threatens us with tortures, I say we shall never bear our heads in safety while Olaf is in life."

The mistrust among the monarchs had to be overcome before they resolved to stay together, raise warriors and fight Olaf who resided at the far end of the lake. Each sovereign sent for enough men to gather a more numerous force than Olaf. But there was a traitor in their midst. At night, Ketil of Ringanes went down with his servants to the water, launched a fine vessel once gifted him by Olaf and rowed with forty armed men to the other end of the lake. With half the men left to guard the boat, he led the others to the King.

Since no time could be lost lest his absence be averted, Ketil hastened straight to Olaf and informed him of the kings' resolution. Olaf recognised the urgency and at once summoned his people. They commandeered all the rowing vessels they could find and set off in calm weather, arriving after evening fell. Thus, they came under cover of darkness and Ketil knew in which houses the rulers slept. They surrounded and guarded these so no-one could escape. The sleepers remained confined there till daylight. The reinforcements had not yet come, so the monarchs did not have enough men to make resistance and they were bound and hauled before Olaf. King Hrorek, the mightiest of the five, was an able and obstinate man whose fidelity he could not trust if he made peace with him. Therefore, Olaf ordered his eyes to be put out. As for Gudrod, he commanded his tongue to be cut out, whereas the other three rulers were relieved to be banished from Norway without mutilation. Those *lendermen* and *bondes* who had taken part in the treacherous plot also succumbed to Olaf's wrath. Some he drove out of the country, some he maimed and with others he made peace.

Olaf took possession of the land of the five monarchs and held hostages from the *lendermen* and *bondes*. Alone, Olaf bore the title of King in Norway.

I made my way to Upsal in the month of Goe, one moon before Yule, meaning to attend the Upsal Thing, which promised to be critical to the future. My visit also provided me with an opportunity to stay with my relatives. To my great surprise, I found Eilaf with our mother.

"Aren't you supposed to be an earl in England?" Such was my greeting.

"And I'm pleased to see you too, brother. Come, dine with us and I'll tell you why I'm here."

Over a sumptuous feast of fresh fish and liberal quantities of ale, Eilaf informed me of events in England. "Soon after he arrived in England, Cnut divided the land into four large earldoms. Mercia, he gave to the serpent Eadric Streona, Ulf. I still know not why. East Anglia went to Thorkell the Tall and that made sense. Northumbria, he handed to Eric of Norway. Again, a sensible choice for Eric is a mighty warrior and leads many men."

"What of Wessex?"

I stared hard at Eilaf, expecting him to declare himself Earl of Wessex, but he made a wry expression.

"That territory Cnut kept for himself."

"So, you got nothing?"

"Not at first, brother. Though you can judge, Cnut's apportionment all followed sound reasoning, except one. There's the point. Eadric could not endure, not with his snake-like character and, true to form, he betrayed Cnut within six months. As I told you when last we met, our sovereign ordered him killed for his trouble and Mercia became divided into smaller earldoms. I am now earl of Western Mercia, which as you know, covers the counties of Hereford, Gloucester, Worcester, Shropshire and Cheshire. It is not the easiest area to govern since there are always conflicts with the Welsh but the land is rich."

"Then I congratulate you, Eilaf."

My brother nodded and began to slice fish from its bone.

"What other news?"

"Cnut married."

"Wasn't he already wed?"

"There's a moot point. He lived with Aelfgifu of Northampton but the Church never recognised their wedding by hand-fasting. He sent her to the north to act as his queen there. To remove the danger of foreign interference, he married Emma of Normandy, Aethelred's widow."

"Very astute. That means he doesn't need to worry about the West Saxon nobility, either."

"True, Ulf, your wife-brother is grown into a formidable ruler. That's why I'm here now. In truth, I should be in Denmark. He sent me to study the political situation here in the northern lands. Rumours reached our shores that Harald does not enjoy good health. I must go in person to Heidaby."

"I don't know about Harald's condition, Eilaf, but I can tell you much of what is happening in Sweden and Norway."

The tale of recent events in Norway shocked my brother. Gratified to receive such a detailed account without moving out of his home, he clapped me on the shoulder and said, "Times are truly changing, Ulf. I shall make sure Cnut is grateful to you for what you are doing. Your wife-brother has a dream of a northern empire under his sway."

"Beware of ambitious schemes, Eilaf. Remember we have seen what Cnut is capable of when he is in difficulty."

Eilaf flushed with anger.

"Always the same old Ulf! Truth be known, you are jealous of my earldom. Why don't you come right out with it?"

"What? Do you believe that? I possess my own land and rank. Why should I envy yours?"

"Because mine is rich, fertile land and yours is full of rock, seaweed and snow."

The argument might have become more heated but the arrival of our widowed mother, looking frail and haggard, induced us to feign brotherly harmony.

When Eilaf sailed for Heidaby, I sat and reflected on our reunion. My sentiments, as ever with Eilaf, were mixed. My brother's place in my heart, I could not deny, was becoming ever more diminished. Ay, I was pleased to see him gone, and in the wider context, relieved that we did not share the same nation and overlord. England might well be a richer land. I was happy to make do with my rocks and seaweed, as Eilaf so contemptuously dismissed my holdings.

Two things troubled me above the rest of his information. Firstly, the state of Harald. I hoped Eilaf would find him hearty because the Baltic states needed the stability he offered. Secondly, could it be that Cnut harboured such imperious plans? Instinct urged me he could not be trusted. From what Eilaf led me to believe, my wife-brother was at the peak of his success at this time. Overweening ambition might prove more than his own undoing. These were my reflections at Yuletide and with hindsight, maybe I underestimated my potential as a seer.

I took my mother into a warm embrace but the discovery of how much flesh had fallen from her bones distressed me. The death of father affected her so deeply and with her offspring so far-flung, she suffered from solitude in addition to the burden of managing our Upsal lands. An idea struck me even as I kissed her brow and released her from my arms.

"Mother, accompany me to Trøndelag. I was going to tell you before I departed, Estrid is heavy with child."

"Oh, my dear son. I shall be a grandmother." Her eyes filled with tears, "How sad your father should not see his grandchild."

"But *you shall* if you travel with me. What say you?"

"Oh, but what of our estate?"

"Mother, you have a host of capable men to take charge of things here. I shall make it my business to speak with them today."

"Then, I will come." Gratified to see the light of enthusiasm, but better, of renewed life, brighten those spent grey eyes, I kissed her cheek and strode off to set about my task.

Without a care in the world, I helped mother out of my ship at the Trøndelag jetty and showed her the improvements made since first setting foot on my lands. Little of it I could claim as my own work since I had been away most of the time. I ushered her into my hall with justifiable pride. But where was Estrid? She did not come to greet us. Was it possible the child was born? It was too soon.

"Estrid! Estrid?"

No reply. Two servants, a married couple, Gunnar and Turid, hastened into the hall.

"Turid. Where is your Mistress?"

"Gone, Lord."

"*Gone?* What do you mean?"

In the face of my temper, poor Turid hung her head and Gunnar stepped forward. The grizzled servant, one of the first to accompany me from Upsal, met my wild eyes.

"Your brother came ten days past to take our Mistress to England."

"Eilaf, here? England! What are you saying, man?"

"He told us he was obeying your instructions, Lord. That Mistresses' brother wished for the child to be delivered in warmer climes." Gunnar gulped, "What were we to think, Lord? He said it was your express will."

"My will! When I lay my hands on Eilaf, better he'd never been born! Sorry, mother!"

My poor mother stood, tears coursing down her cheeks, and I was hard-pressed to understand her feeble utterances.

"Whatever possessed him to expose Estrid to such a hazardous crossing at this time of year?"

"Mother, I must leave at once for England. Stay here and make it your home. My servants will tend to your every need."

I glared at Turid who nodded dumbly.

"I shall not! I'm coming with you," Mother replied with some of her former spirit. "I shall see my grandchild born and prevent you from any act of folly."

When mother determined on something, nothing could make her change her mind. If a man like Thorgils, my father, could not prevail when her will was set, what hope had I? Within the hour we had cast off and were headed across the open sea for England.

My thoughts veered from the murderous to the regretful. I should be in Norway at the court of Olaf at this critical time in Norwegian-Swedish relations. The rough sea and the freezing spray, soaking me to the skin, cooled my temper. The true motive for Eilaf's unexpected conduct eluded me at this moment. Besides, the navigation in these harsh winter conditions gave me more than enough to worry about. To say I was relieved when the familiar sight of the Thanet ness appeared off to starboard is an understatement. We rounded Kent and headed directly for Sussex, whence we would travel overland to Winchester. I wagered all on Cnut holding court there and I was right.

To be fair to the fellow, he received us with the utmost grace and assured me that his sister Estrid enjoyed the warmest and most luxurious chamber in the palace.

"You will want to greet your wife at once, but tell me Ulf, what possessed you to send her to England in her delicate state in such a perilous season?"

The hostile tone of the accusation and its injustice lent an unwise sharpness to my voice. After all, I was addressing a powerful monarch.

"*I?* The first I knew of this was when I found Estrid gone from my hearth! My servants told me Eilaf referred to the voyage as determined by your will, Cnut."

"Mine?" He fairly roared the word. "Then this is all of Eilaf's doing, I assure you. Lucky for him he is in Mercia now. What can be the meaning of this?"

"It is what I have been asking myself, lord, these last few days."

Cnut rose smiling and laid a hand on my arm, "Fear not, Ulf, our Estrid will have the best of care. Your child will be delivered safe and hale."

Thus it was that Sweyn Estridson, a man with a splendid future, came squalling into the world one moon later. For the moment, the little fellow, suckling at his mother's breast, was the greatest delight of my life. His uncle, Eilaf, on the other hand, remained a dark distant shadow, safe from my wrath in Mercia. I suppose in my lighter moments, I might have recognised to him the superior comfort of the English court for my loved ones. I confess, my brooding at his high-handed conduct and my desire to be at the side of Olaf distorted my reasoning.

Part of me wanted to go to Mercia to confront Eilaf but again my wish to be in Norway prevailed. Estrid sensibly refused to put our babe at risk of the winter crossing and promised to come home in the calm weather of summer. I expected my mother to accompany me but she too declined, preferring to remain with her infant grandson.

Accordingly, I went to inform Cnut of my departure and found him in high spirits. He had created two new earldoms in Wessex and much satisfied, confided in me that he now felt secure enough to dismiss the fleet that had brought him to England.

"A good one-off payment ought to settle the matter, Ulf. As your wife-brother, I hope you will support my interests. Do you know that my brother Harald does not enjoy the best of health?"

"I confess to hearing something of the kind."

"It's true. Should anything happen to him, I, as next in line will take the throne. There may be a time when I shall need trusted friends to look after my interests in Denmark. Might you be such a man for me, Ulf?"

I assured him of my good faith, which was the truth at that moment, and took my leave for the voyage to Norway. The fresh air of the North Sea set me to thinking. Why had Eilaf behaved in such a way? What had he gained from luring me to England? Although the sea was not shrouded in winter fog, my understanding was no clearer. Among the conjectures I dismissed, resurfaced the insistent thought that it might have had something to do with Cnut's parting discussion. Later, I was to realise how close I had come on this crossing to comprehending his motives.

Joy at the birth of my son and my purpose in returning to Norway overrode what had become a mild rancour at my brother's untoward action. Since all had gone well, there was no point in dwelling on the danger into which he had placed my wife and then unborn child. I shrugged off my resentment until a time when I would come face to face with Eilaf and confront him. For the present, there were other matters of graver importance to occupy my attention.

17

ULLARAKER, SWEDEN, 1018

After two days assessing the situation at Upsal, I hastened to Ingegerd's farm to where Jarl Ragnvald, Bjorn and Hjalte had repaired, far from the indiscreet ears of the court. The purpose of the visit was to convince Olof's daughter to accept Olaf the Thick's proposal of matrimony. They impressed Ingegerd with how in one night, Olaf had taken five monarchs prisoners, deprived them of their lands and seized their kingdoms. By the time I arrived, the work of persuasion was done with Ingegerd replying positively but imposing the condition of her father's assent.

In the following days, we discussed the way this might be obtained. Jarl Ragnvald suggested a plan to involve one of the influential *lagmen* of Tinnaland: Lagman Thorgny. Not only was he related to the Jarl but also once brought him up as his foster-father. This idea appealed so much that I decided to accompany Ragnvald into Tinnaland. Thorgny was old and presided over a grand court. His followers told me eagerly that he was considered one of the wisest men in Sweden.

Thorgny's house was a magnificent structure and, when we entered, there were many people. In the high seat sat an old man – I had never seen one so stout. His beard was so long that it lay like a white pelt on his knee and spread over his whole chest. In spite of this, his appearance was handsome and stately.

We advanced to his throne, where he greeted us in a jovial and kindly manner. I had hoped to come straight to the point of our visit but Ragnvald knew best how to handle the matter. After three days, he began to explain how Olaf had sent me to conclude a peace agreement. He spoke at length about what injury it was to the people of Gautland that there was hostility between the two kingdoms. Adding that Olaf had dispatched other ambassadors to address Olof Eirikson, he outlined the problem.

"The Swede, Olof, takes the business so grievously that he has uttered menaces against those who entertain it. So it is, my foster-father, that I do not trust myself in this affair. I visit you to obtain good counsel and help from you in this regard."

Thorgny frowned and sat in silence for so long that I feared he might not aid us. To my relief, at last he said, "I must go to the Upsal Thing and give you such assistance that you may speak freely before the King."

We thanked Thorgny and accompanied him to the moot.

In the vast hall at Upsal, the sovereign occupied a stool with his court standing in a circle around him. Opposite him sat Jarl Ragnvald, Thorgny and myself. Behind them in a ring stood the *bonde* community. After the usual business of the Thing was settled, the marshal Bjorn arose and positioned himself beside the Jarl's stool.

"Olaf sends me here with the message that he will offer to the Swedish people peace and the frontiers that in old times were fixed between Norway and Sweden."

The King sprang to his feet, "Be silent!" he bellowed, "For such speeches are useless."

Thereupon, Bjorn sat and Ragnvald rose, "Sire, the people of Gautland send their entreaty to you to make peace with the Norse ruler. They suffer deprivations, with no salt to cure their food so it perishes in the autumn and in the winter they starve. No herrings arrive from Norway as of wont, making their condition intolerable. They must go without all things from Norway necessary to their households. Also, they are exposed to attack and hostility whenever the Norsemen gather an army and make an inroad on them. Olaf has sent men hither with the intent to obtain Ingegerd's hand in marriage."

I believe Ragnvald could have done no more for our cause, but my heart sank at the wrath on the Swedish King's countenance.

"I will not listen to proposals of peace from the fat man. Also Jarl, you, whom I trust, should never have entered into a peaceful truce with such a fellow. In truth, I consider it treason. You deserve to be driven forth from this realm. I put this behaviour down to the interference of your spouse, Ingebjorg. What an unhappy alliance! Imprudent of you, my friend to take up with such a wife."

Ragnvald grew pale at this shower of insults and in the whole hall not a sound was to be heard as everyone dwelt on the gravity of the speech.

I feared bloodshed but Thorgny heaved his bulk off his stool and other *bondes* rushed together from all parts to stand near him to sustain and listen to his words of wisdom.

To begin with, he spoke of the disposition of previous Swedish monarchs. In truth, his speech bored me for I was not familiar with the names and connections. But one name caught my attention – Eirik the Victorious – who enlarged the Swedish dominion and yet, said Thorgny, he was easy and agreeable to listen to the opinions of others. The implicit criticism of the present ruler was clear to all but now came a heavy and open reproach.

"The King who reigns now allows no man to presume to talk with him unless it be what he desires to hear. On this alone he applies all his power, while he permits the tax-paying lands in other countries to slip away from him through laziness and weakness. He wants to lay Norway under him, which no Swedish monarch before him ever desired, and therewith brings war and distress on many a man. Now it is our will, we *bondes*, that you Olof, make peace with the

Norsemen and wed your daughter, Ingegerd, with Olaf the Thick." Lagman Thorgny waited for the din of assent to die down, before continuing, "Sire, you ought to re-conquer the kingdoms in the east countries which your relations and forefathers held. In this purpose alone will we follow you into war. If you will not do what we desire, we will attack you and put you to death. We will no longer suffer law and peace to be disturbed or the insupportable pride you show towards us. Now, make haste, tell us what resolution you will take."

I, like everyone around me, reached for my sword amid the din of approval at this speech and the clash of arms and shouting.

Pale-faced, Olof Eirikson stood and began, "All Swedish monarchs have allowed the *bondes* to rule in all according to their will. I am no different."

Weapons sheathed, the clamour subsided and talk of a truce and reconciliation commenced. The Thing resolved that Ingegerd should wed Olaf Haraldson and the contract feast would be arranged by Jarl Ragnvald. Nothing now impeded our return to Gautland, where Bjorn, Hjalte and I stayed with the Jarl for some days. Thence, we travelled into Norway to deliver the news to Olaf of the successful outcome of our mission.

We journeyed as far as Tunsberg where Olaf had taken residence for Easter. To this port came many merchant vessels from Saxony, Iceland, and Russia but also some from England. In this way, the sad news of the death of Harald of Denmark reached us. Cnut was his successor but he was across the North Sea ruling over another realm. This was the first of several bad tidings to blight our happiness and dampen our enthusiasm for a brighter, more peaceful future. In Denmark, with no sovereign to control the Danish chieftains, they grew restless and began to prepare for a revival of Viking enterprise. Such pillaging in his new kingdom Cnut would never tolerate. I did not doubt that these same rumours would have reached him in Wessex.

We consoled ourselves that with Denmark in turmoil, we had at least brought peace to Norway and Sweden. To set the seal on this, in the summer Olaf led us to the frontier with Sweden to a place named Konungahella where the wedding was to be held. We waited a long time for the Swedish bridal party to come but there was no sign of them. Did Olof Eirikson mean to break his word?

He did. Unable to swallow his resentment for having consent forced out of him at the Upsal Thing, Olof informed his daughter he would never accept such a marriage. Distressed, Ingegerd, aware of the threat from Norway the Gautlanders would face, told Jarl Ragnvald. In turn, he begged Olaf not to pillage his lands since he and his people had worked for a different, happier outcome. The Norse King discussed this in a hastily assembled Thing and conceded the truth of Ragnvald's assertion. As a result, Olaf disbanded his forces. He also proclaimed that the next summer he meant to call men from all over the land to march on Olof Eirikson and punish him for his want of faith. The storm clouds thus gathered over the Baltic. Olaf returned to Viken and released me to return to my wife and little Sweyn in Trøndelag. A strange mixture of joyfulness and heavy-heartedness accompanied me on my homeward journey.

18

HUSABY, VASTERGOTLAND, AUTUMN 1019-SUMMER 1020 AD

The situation in 1019 in the northern waters was one of widespread chaos and gloomy forecast. With news from England that Cnut was preparing an expedition to Denmark, the Danish Vikings gathered to pillage in the Baltic as an alternative to incursions across the North Sea.

Domestic bliss could not quell my anxieties and mood swings; therefore, at Michaelmas, I decided to leave Trøndelag until a more secure future might be created for my family. Unclear as to my part in helping to assure this prospect I acted, as ever, in the belief that my destiny was inextricably bound to that of Norway. My overriding ambition was to foster stability in the region.

To what do I attribute moodiness? A state of mental confusion, I suppose. Acutely aware of being different from my fellow men, I had to reflect on what was meaningful to me. Here am I, a Swede, living in Norway and serving a Danish king – when I'm not serving a Norwegian. I was happy, or so I thought, confident I could sustain the happiness by living for the day. I no longer felt the need to accumulate wealth but instead relied on reason to guide me towards the goal

I aspired to. I wanted to help create a peaceful co-existence for the men of the North. After all, what more did I need? Apart from peace, I had everything I could ever want. Except orientation.

There was a necessary layer of order, direction and meaning I needed to add to rise above my warrior's existence. Intuition led me to believe that life is best conducted in a place between safety and danger. To achieve my goal required quiet commitment, respectful engagement and a love of something greater than oneself. I saw it in the eyes of bishop Grimkel. But whatever inspired him would not serve me, since my prayers fell on deaf ears. With no spiritual armour to strengthen me, I must nevertheless risk harm for what I believed in.

Some would say my belief was irrational. Yet, from the point of view of survival, I cannot think of anything more rational than finding something worthwhile to live for. Should that not be a peaceful society for my little son to grow up in? A community sustained by the trustworthiness of its rulers: what better purpose might I seek? It was clear that I had stumbled towards this aim with uncertain steps and with no real sense of direction. Betrayal, violation, killings and starvation, I have experienced them all and am weary of them. My life must be dedicated to a more noble end.

In summary, I could say I may not know in my mind where I was going, but proof will be provided through the doing.

Although my instincts urged me away from those I loved in Trøndelag, I was unsure where to go. King Olaf's court ought to be the logical choice but the more I reflected on it, the less sure I became. Olaf's main preoccupation of late was religion, with his mission to Christianise the northern lands. I did not share his enthusiasm, laudable as the Church might find it. Where then should I journey and to what useful purpose?

The most loyal and influential man I ever met, and somebody whom I considered a friend, would receive me with a warm welcome. I also admired the sageness of Jarl Ragnvald, so I decided to go with eight companions to his court at Husaby by the vast lake, Vänern. This area of Sweden, Vastergotland, was the only part of the country free from pagan worship. They say that King Olaf was baptised at the well next to the wooden church at Husaby in 1008. I believed this to be true and looked forward to seeing the Jarl's lakeside estates for the first time.

As imagined, I received a generous welcome and the meal of freshly-baked rye bread and pan-fried smelt direct from the waters of the Vänern was delicious. How strange the weavings of fate! It brought me to Husaby at the same time as a beautiful woman and at the moment of the arrival of startling news. The former was the daughter of Olof Eirikson by an Obotitian mistress, Edia. This dark-eyed beauty had suffered ill-treatment from her stepmother and so lived with foster parents in Vastergotland. Her kind, sweet, artless nature made her well-liked by all. I too fell under her spell. The region of her upbringing meant she had embraced Christianity.

The news brought to Husaby was that the Kiev-Rus King, Jarisleif the Wise, had come to the Swedish court to ask for the hand of Ingegerd. His suit was accepted and a wedding date fixed. At these tidings Ragnvald paled and trembled. Not only was he out of favour with Olof Eirikson but was also now in peril from Olaf the Thick. The Norwegian monarch would not take kindly to such a blow to his pride. Ragnvald had failed in a spectacular manner to arrange and complete the wedding the King desired so ardently.

"My life is not worth a fishbone, Ulf!"

I sought to console him and promised to intervene with Olaf in his favour. In truth, I feared any similar action on my part would be ineffectual. In any case, I believed the greater danger to Ragnvald came from the Swede, Olof, whose vengeful, proud nature was known to everyone.

The solution for Olaf was under our noses but, as often happens, the obvious at first goes unnoticed. My best ideas come when I wake in the morning, my brain rested and fresh. So, the morning after we received the news of Ingegerd's betrothal, I dressed in haste and hurried to find Ragnvald. I thought it better not to make a move until

I had consulted the wise jarl. The light of renewed hope brightening his countenance when I put my idea to him gratified me.

"Ulf! This might work! Well done, my friend. Set about it then!"

Astrid had an abundance of regal qualities. Why should her illegitimacy count against her? Royal blood still coursed through her veins. With these thoughts occupying my mind, I sought her out in private. I began by extolling the virtues of King Olaf, liberally laced with tales of his deeds and the excellence of his conversion of Norwegians, Icelanders and islanders. How could she fail to be impressed? What heartened me most, however, was her absolute refusal to countenance an approach to Olof for his blessing.

"No, Lord Ulf, if this marriage is to go ahead it will be by my consent alone."

"Then, Lady, you will permit me to raise the matter with our King Olaf?"

Her dark eyes opened wider and she gave me a girlish smile, although I guessed her age to be on a par with mine.

"Queen of Norway. The title pleases me. Pray, speak well of me to Olaf."

"My Lady, your virtues and comeliness make it impossible to do otherwise. Forgive me but I must prepare to travel to Sarpsborg, where he resides for the Yule festivities. As soon as I receive his reply I will return."

She favoured me with a sweet and hopeful smile causing my heart to soar. I left convinced that Astrid would make the perfect bride for Olaf and Queen for Norway.

The bitter winter journey through grandiose scenery brought me to a realisation of the futility of our everyday strivings. Confronted by the majesty of nature and its unrelenting severity, ice in our beards and grateful for the thick fleece covering our clothing, the overriding sensation was of separateness. Detachment from other living beings whilst inexplicably being in unity with everything hardly made sense.

The clearness of the air on our second day out made the snow seem whiter than our eyes could bear but when night fell, it brought the most ethereal green glow to the sky. I had not experienced the Northern Lights before and must confess that the fronds in the sky and the malachite flames licking the horizon troubled my new faith. The old religion called it Bifröst, the celestial bridge from Earth to the gods. At least it provided an explanation for the awesome spectacle. My Christian faith would, I suppose, attribute it to a marvel of God the Creator. I struggle to understand it myself, without attempting to explain the countless wonders of Nature around me. Why, I wondered, might a rock-face split open and a spring gush forth from it?

How fortunate we had been to benefit from clear air to marvel at the sky because on the third day, bad weather set in, bringing three days of dispiriting mist. The chilly air penetrated to the bones and it was a hard task to stop the hands and feet becoming completely numb. On the second of these days, we came across a group of men stretching out nets by a mere, checking them for their repair and strength.

They seemed to be in an animated discussion and my curiosity was aroused when one of them pointed to a white standing stone and their gesticulations increased. On hailing and approaching them, they treated our arrival as most opportune. They told us we could help them avenge the death of a young brother, whose drowned corpse lay cold and pallid on the ground.

"A fishing accident?" I asked.

"Fishing? Would that it were so simple."

"What then?"

"This is the work of the Alva who frequents this place and comes out when there's mist."

"An elfin creature?"

I was a Christian and no longer gave credence to heathen beliefs. The earnestness of these simple fisher folk, the remoteness of the mere and the ethereal nature of the damp air swirling suspended over the water, made me shiver with apprehension.

"Ay. Look at our Leif," he indicated the body of the handsome youth. "She *lured him* to his death and he's not the first hereabouts – but he's the first in my lifetime. We'll put an end to her seductions once and for all."

The other men stared at us, as people do at outsiders, to gauge our reactions.

"How do you mean to capture an elf?" I asked.

"I say she lives under yon stone," he pointed to the upright white stone, which, when I thought about it, had an eerie, out-of-place appearance. "Can your men lend a hand to uproot it?" he asked.

"What do you think to find under it?"

"Can't rightly say. A doorway? Stairs? We'll only know when we shift it."

"Right then, lads, let's set about it!" I called.

"You others stand by with the nets," the swarthy fellow ordered, "to catch the fleet-footed Alva," he said by way of explanation.

His muscled, knotted arms were the first laid on the stone and, together, we lent our weight and strength to his efforts. In spite of the combined might of seven men, the stone did not move an inch.

"Curse the *Dis*-creature," the fisherman cried, "she's cast a spell on the stone. No man can ever defeat her magic to shift it."

He used the ancient term *Dis* to describe a female spirit of the mist.

"Let it be! It's useless. We must learn from this disgrace not ever to venture out in misty weather. Thanks for your help, all the same."

He continued by inviting us back to his home for a warming drink but I refused as I wished to press on before darkness came. Overcoming his protestations and resisting the allure of warmth and refreshment, we pressed on.

Lars, one of my thegns, drew close to me. From Lars, as a lad, I had bought my first knife.

"What are we to think about that business back there, Lord?"

"What is there to think, Lars? Our religion condemns superstitious beliefs. There are no elves. It is foolish fancy. The poor fellow met with an accident that drowned him. At times, fear of the unknown acts on our minds and makes us invent the most improbable fancies."

Lars made the sign of the Cross.

"It makes me feel better to think there are no supernatural beings," he sighed.

"Angels and devils are enough for anyone," I told him, convinced in any case there was more to the world than met the eye. The magnificence of Nature we had so recently witnessed could not be taken for granted. Our poor aching, blistered feet confirmed this thought. We were but specks on the grandiose tapestry of Nature.

I will not pretend otherwise than it came as a mental and physical relief when we reached our destination. The warmth of our welcome compensated for the hardships undergone on our journey.

"Well met, Lord Ulf! We sorely felt your absence. How fare your wife and son?"

"Well, I thank you, Sire."

"I sense you are eager to tell me something more, am I right?"

"Your acute observation does not fail you, Lord. But it is best we speak alone if it pleases you."

Olaf led me to an empty room and listened with mounting enthusiasm to my descriptions of Lady Astrid.

"Her eyes are like two dark pools, you say? What of her voice, Ulf, is it sweet?"

"As that of a nightingale, Lord."

Our exchanges continued in this vein for some time, until satisfied, Olaf's face darkened.

"I will not be made a fool of again, Jarl Ulf."

"Sire?"

"I will not tolerate another disappointment, is that clear?"

Clearer than the venomous expression on his countenance was hard to imagine. I gulped and blurted,

"There will be no displeasure, my King."

"Make sure there is not, Ulf or you will rue the day."

As sudden as a sea squall dies down, Olaf's face brightened.

"Come, we must toast to my new intended."

I did not enjoy the drinks and my anxiety that Astrid might change her mind weighed too much on me. Was she the fickle kind? The idea was difficult to entertain. If she proved whimsical, I would flee to Denmark. But what of my family?

"Ulf, you look pale."

"Nought, Lord. I caught a chill and it upsets my stomach."

"Better drink another then," Olaf was an unsound physician. "You must take many gifts to Astrid, Ulf. She must think me the most generous of men. When do you leave? On the morrow?"

I gave him a wry smile, "If my stomach permits, Sire."

"Make sure it does, Ulf. My patience has its limits."

"I am sure it will be well, Lord."

I felt colour returning to my cheeks. The thought that Olaf would shower Astrid with fine offerings could only help my mission.

"I will bring your betrothed after the Yule feast, Sire."

"It's best."

I departed in better spirits, which despite the bitter cold of the snow-laden wind kept me warm.

They soared to new heights at Husaby, where conceding scarcely the time to hear of my arrival, Astrid came in haste to determine Olaf's intentions.

"Lord Ulf, what did the King say to your proposal?"

I feigned a sour face for the pleasure of teasing.

"Oh," she lowered her head.

I laughed and waved a hand at two of my retinue who hastened to carry the chest containing Olaf's gifts.

"Then it was but a wonderful dream," Astrid murmured.

"And it still is, my Lady," I grinned. "Can you not see, I tease you? Look, these are the presents our sovereign sends to express his delight at your consent."

My men opened the chest and flung back the heavy lid so Astrid slunk towards the contents lithe as a mountain cat. Like that creature, her claws seized on a fur stole – as white as a swan's breast – the softest ermine. She pressed it to her face, nuzzling into its downy depths.

"It's so silken!" she cried, her girlish enthusiasm captivating us all as she moved from the fur to the jewels and the gowns. Olaf had chosen well. "I love him though I've never met him!"

The last of my worries melted with the snow on my boots. Exchanging a wide smile with Jarl Ragnvald, I said, "My friend, we can enjoy the festivities of Christ's Mass and make preparations to go to Sarpsborg when it is ended."

"Ay," and the Jarl laid an avuncular hand on Astrid's arm. We shall have you wed to Olaf by Candlemas, my dear."

The magic atmosphere of Yuletide behind us, we set off for Olaf's winter quarters with an escort of one hundred and twenty armed men. Jarl Ragnvald meant to take no risks with Astrid's welfare. In Sarpsborg, Olaf had prepared every detail. With many notables invited to the wedding, he had spared no expense on fine liquors and food.

The meeting of Astrid and Olaf removed my last anxiety – that one might not like the other. I need not have fretted; they took to each other as if they had been childhood sweethearts. Jarl Ragnvald drew up the marriage contract with the same dowry at the time settled on Ingegerd. While Olaf consented to the same bridal gift agreed upon for Astrid's step-sister. Thus, the matrimony proceeded without obstacle and Olaf and Norway boasted a new and radiant Queen.

The only blight on our happiness arrived from the Swedish court whence our informant brought news of Olof Eirikson's reaction to the marriage. In a towering rage, he declared Ragnvald a traitor who had given his daughter as a concubine to the enemy and announced he meant to hang him. Of little import that Olof had ignored the existence of Astrid for years, the threat was only too real. It pained me to see Ragnvald so worried. Of course he was safe in Norway, but as things stood to go back to his home in Gautland meant risking death.

Ingegerd saved him. In the most astute manner, she made his

well-being a condition of her marriage to Jarisleif. First, she asked her intended husband for the gift of the town of Ladoga, which he conceded to her, and then that Ragnvald be made Earl of the territory. This he granted too and when Ragnvald transferred to his new Russian earldom, he was safe from the wrath of Olof.

Sadly, we could not state that the wedding of Olaf to Astrid procured peace between their two countries. The nature of Olof made this auspicious outcome improbable. Still, for the moment, Olof confined himself to brooding so that trouble in the Baltic came from another quarter.

Cnut, whose arrival with a large fleet some months before seemed to have calmed the Danish malcontents, had to invade Pomerania. There, the Wends collaborating with Danish dissidents planned to usurp his throne. Thanks to a brilliant night-time raid on the Wendish encampment by Earl Godwin, Cnut won a notable victory. These events affected me directly. A messenger arrived at the court of Olaf from Cnut beseeching my presence in Heidaby. I was so well entrenched in the good graces of Olaf that he willingly released me with assurances of his goodwill to Cnut. Given his victory at Nesjar, this, with a gift of a splendid gold arm-ring, would not go amiss.

As I travelled, my mind was troubled by what Cnut might want of me. My concern was that he should not seek to detach my loyalty from Olaf. I had no intention of turning my back on a friend, my adopted monarch.

"Ulf, do you know why I called you to me?"

"I have no idea, Sire."

"You will have heard of my troubles with the Wends and certain Danish lords?"

"I have."

"For the moment, they are no longer a problem. I dealt with the Wends and confiscated the lands of the exiled lords. But my overseas possessions need me, Ulf. I fear betrayal in England. It is hardly by chance that the traitors turned to the Wends. There is a serpent at my bosom in England and I refer to Thorkell the Tall."

"Surely not, Lord."

"Do not contradict me, Ulf."

A dangerous glint came to Cnut's eye so I mollified him.

"True, Thorkell is not new to duplicity."

He grunted and placed a hand on my arm.

"Which is why I need you, brother."

Charmed by the use of the affectionate term referring to our kinship through my marriage with his sister, I smiled.

"You wish me to slay Thorkell?"

It was Cnut's turn to be shocked.

"Even if I wished it, Ulf, I think it would be a very hard task for you to accomplish. Nay, Thorkell is mine to deal with."

His brow furrowed and he looked careworn.

"What then, is it that you want of me, Lord?"

"Ulf, you shall be Regent of Denmark in my absence. Come with me to yonder bedchamber."

I followed him, my mind awhirl at this unexpected turn of events. In a trance, I barely registered the small figure asleep on the bed.

"Meet Harthacnut, the Crown Prince of Denmark and your ward. I am entrusting the boy to you, Ulf. You will protect him with your life and serve his best interests.

I stared with tenderness at the silken locks of the golden-haired, angelic form at repose and knew that it would be so. The infant was but some moons older than my Sweyn. They would be playmates.

I bowed to Cnut, "Lord, it is a great honour and responsibility you bestow on me. I shall do my utmost to merit your faith."

"I know, Ulf. Who better for this purpose? You are in close friendship with the King of Norway and with the Queen of Russia. In spite of being a Swede, beware of your own people and of the Danes too. But I trust you will succeed."

A memory pricked me to say, "What of you, Sire? Have you

151

renounced your interests in the north?" Cnut seemed stung by this remark.

"Not in the slightest. God has chosen me to fulfil great achievements. I know this." But he did not elaborate. Perhaps this was as well, or I should have begun the Regency in quite a different spirit.

19

HEIDABY, WINTER 1020 - 1022 AD

Life is like a long, weary, Norwegian winter's night; intolerable but for flashes of light brought by occasional flares of love – reflected in Estrid's eyes or on seeing little Sweyn and his playmate Harthacnut tottering in infant embraces. These were the moments that brightened the deepening gloom enfolding me. Why should grim thoughts engulf a man who has everything? It is tempting to exert power over men and to shine but this has its perils. I strived for pre-eminence only for the sake of good, and refused to be obsessed and numbed by dominance for its own ends. Would that it were so for those others who influence our existence.

My predicament was unenviable but to some extent, I had myself to blame. King Olaf of Norway was my friend and I had served him faithfully but can a man obey two masters? I ought to have repulsed Cnut's request to serve as Regent for Harthacnut. A sense of familial duty urged me to accept where refusal would have been the wiser course. Or had it? Cnut was not a man to be gainsaid or trifled with.

Whereas I once was ignorant of events in the northern lands, I was by this point aware of every political palpitation, each moment of domestic crisis. Rather than being reassured by knowledge, my understanding of the dark nature contained within every individual and the potential consequences of unleashing it on the world made me suffer. The Church would have King Olaf a saint for imposing Christianity throughout the North. Others shared my insight into the despicable core of his soul. For every baptism effected, did he not have a string of murders and mutilations on his conscience? Was not the most recent the murder of Olver of Eggja? In the interior of the Throndhjem land, the custom was to offer sacrifice in autumn for a good winter. Olver had to get the feast in order. King Olaf took three hundred men, went in the night to Maerin and surrounded Olver's house with armed men. The monarch ordered an atrocious death for Olver and many other men there before taking all the provisions for the feast, then had these provisions taken to his ships. The King also let all the *bondes* he believed had the greatest part in the heathen arrangements be plundered by his men. Some were seized and placed in irons, others fled and many were robbed of their possessions.

Thereafter other *bondes* were summoned to a Thing; but since many powerful men were prisoners, their friends and relations resolved to promise obedience to Olaf. Thus, he brought the people back to *the right faith*, gave them teachers and constructed and consecrated churches. The King took Olver's lands and land of the others who he judged most guilty; some he had executed, others maimed, some driven out of the country, and he imposed fines on others. Then he returned to winter in Nidaros.

This is King Olaf. Is he a man I could cross by serving Cnut?

And what about Cnut? He bound men to him by means other than bloodshed but just as effective. He gave my sister, Gytha, in wedlock to the mightiest Saxon nobleman, Earl Godwin. By basing his dominance around large towns and great men then binding ecclesiastical organisation to this control, Cnut wrested power out of the hands of the local overlords. That is not to say he would not resort to violence if crossed. Quite the opposite, as the disappearance of those foolhardy enough to challenge him clearly showed. Cnut now ruled over a settled kingdom and his influence was spreading northwards into Scotland. His words to me suggested his eyes turned to Denmark and, worse as far as I was concerned, to Norway also. If I was right, where would that leave me?

My father made me swear *'to eschew treachery all my life'* and in this I have done my best. What must I do should it come to war between Olaf and Cnut?

I gained respite from mental turmoil by engaging in everyday tasks. Scrambling along the rocky shore with Estrid to check the sea otter traps, I turned my ankle. On a flat rock, I unlaced my boot, took it off and massaged my aching joint.

"Ulf! look!"

The excitement and urgency in Estrid's voice made me follow the line of her pointing finger to a speck bobbing in the distance of the estuary to seaward.

"Isn't that the black raven?"

There was no doubt in her voice. Her certainty was born of having the sharpest eyes in Heidaby. Only some minutes later could I confirm her sighting as the agile long-ship, driven by a full sail of wind, bore into the range of my eyesight. The insignia meant Eilaf was approaching. But why? Once more my thoughts plunged and raced like a waterfall over a cliff in winter. He should be in England fulfilling his duties to Cnut. What could his surprise arrival mean? Only a matter of importance would bring him across the North Sea in this season. Why was he coming in on the Baltic coast? He must have sailed around the peninsula. Was all well between him and Cnut? Was he fleeing into exile? These were the wild, muddled thoughts assailing me as I struggled to lace up my boot on the slippery rock.

"Let me help you."

I confess to leaning on Estrid as I hobbled home, swearing at my slow progress, all notions of checking otter traps driven away by the unexpected appearance of Eilaf's ship. I wanted to be home and seated in stately splendour to receive him. Had he come to see his brother or the Regent of Denmark? Soon would I know.

"Brother, how good to see you well. And little Sweyn! I swear you are the image of your grandfather! All you need is a forked beard, little man!"

He ruffled the hair of his nephew and bent to embrace him.

"Ow! Steady on! I yield!"

Eilaf eased away the tiny fingers tugging at his plaited whiskers and turned his attention to Estrid and Harthacnut.

I cut across the pleasantries:

"You are welcome to our home brother. Forgive my curiosity; what brings you away from the lush fields of Mercia? Are you in trouble?"

"Trouble? It depends what you mean by that, Ulf. I come with warnings and advice."

"How so? But come, be seated. You must be hungry and have a thirst."

No sooner were the words uttered than Estrid sprang to her duty as hostess with sharp commands.

"You treat yourself well, Ulf, I swear your ale is the best I've ever tasted."

"Or your thirst is the greatest in Denmark," I laughed.

Eilaf licked his lips and wiped the foam from his thick moustache. His handsome features changed to a serious expression.

"Ulf, I have come to warn you and to enlist your aid."

His eyes searched my face to judge my reaction, which for the moment was curiosity alone.

"You will remember that Cnut attacked Pomerania last year."

"Of course."

"Do you know why?"

The question, frankly, surprised me. Did he know something I did not?

"Because the Jutland lords in opposition to Cnut allied with the Wends."

"Have you thought to ask why they joined together?"

"Where is this leading, Eilaf?"

"You never were the patient kind, Ulf. Hark! Thorkell quarrelled with Cnut."

"Did Cnut not make him earl?"

"He did. But the kernel of the issue is Cnut's ambition. Ulf, he has banished Thorkell."

"You will not lose sleep over that, brother, as I remember you were anything but friends with Thorkell the Tall."

"That rift was bridged long ago. Now we have the same interests and they lie in Sweden. I too have quarrelled with Cnut."

"With your King? Are you banished too?"

Were my thoughts on the shore of the estuary when I first sighted his vessel to be proved right?

"I am not. But something has to be done."

"About what exactly?"

"Cnut dreams of a northern empire. He is not satisfied with being King of England and Denmark. His avid gaze turns to Sweden and Norway."

"What proof do you have of this?"

"Do you not see what is happening across the water so close to home? Cast your eyes to Lund. There, Cnut has established his supremacy, setting up his own man and installing a bishop. His aim is to control the Oresund and its trade routes from there. He is at present consolidating his power in Skåne. Ulf, he is using the same methods that have brought him dominion in England. It is but a small step from Skåne to Upsal and our possessions. That is why Cnut and Thorkell argued. Thorkell's wife-brother has been dispossessed in Skåne. Hence the unrest of the Wends, driven by their love of Thorkell. I am come to awaken you. Cnut is on a collision course not only with the King of Sweden but also with your friend King Olaf of Norway."

This made me sit up.

"What do you know of Cnut's dealings with Olaf?"

"This past winter Olaf has pushed as far north as Halgoland and by dint of sword and fire converted the northern region to Christianity. There is much unrest there and Cnut, profiting by it, has received two offended Norse lords into his English court. Thence, he dispatched ambassadors to Olaf, asserting his ancient right to the throne of Norway and offering Olaf peace and the kingdom in fief if he swore allegiance to him. Olaf sent them packing and Cnut prepares for war. What will you do, Ulf?"

My brother, knowing me so well, read the desperation in my countenance. Olaf accepting Cnut as overlord was unthinkable.

"What will *you* do, Eilaf?"

He frowned and scowled at the ale in his hand.

"I will resist him. No one man can rule over all these lands. When a family has held certain estates for many lifetimes, it is unjust that they are taken away to suit the ambitions of one man. Ulf, that fate awaits us if we do not withstand Cnut's designs."

"Are you asking me to betray my King?"

"Not to betray but to resist him."

"Are they not one and the same thing?"

"Ulf, I knew your stiffness would be the ruin of us!"

"Brother, let us not be hasty. Let us not quarrel. You have given me much to think about and I am ever bound to the oath we took to our father. Remember: *'swear you will eschew treachery all your lives and sustain one another, when in need'*."

"I do not forget. But, Ulf, now *is* a time of need."

"Then I promise you, brother, I will ponder upon your words and take action as I see fit."

"That is all I ask."

Eilaf relaxed visibly before my eyes and his features returned to the roguish friendliness that so endeared him to everyone. I felt compelled to win his amiability:

"My thanks that you have come to warn me. You see too well my predicament."

In an unusual gesture of warmth, Eilaf took my hand across the table and squeezed it.

"Take care, brother, soon things will come to a head and you will be in the shield-wall."

How prophetic these words were to be. A few weeks after they were uttered, news came from Sweden that King Olof had died a natural death in his bed. His young son, Anund Jacob, succeeded him. If I am to be honest, this death came as a relief. Kings Olaf and Olof had, at last, made peace but it was common knowledge that it was forced upon Olof the Swede by his subjects. They also constrained him to share his rule with his son. I'm ashamed to confess to being glad to see the end of this arrogant, inflexible tyrant who had caused so much suffering to me and his own people. Paradoxically, had he lived, events might well have taken an easier course for me and for my country. I wish I could say that Eilaf and I parted on the best of terms. But not so. As the days passed without a decision from me, his irritation grew apace until he confronted me.

"What am I to do? I have sworn to Cnut that I will protect Harthacnut and rule in the best interests of his son. This I will do or die in the attempt."

"It may well come to your death, Ulf. If you have need of me, call. You will find me in Upsal."

"Will you not return to your duties in England?"

"Not until Cnut is forced to see sense. Dark days lie ahead, brother."

With these words, he bade his farewell and ignored my call to turn back. I presumed he was in Upsal.

20

HEIDABY 1022 AD

Four men swaggered into my hall and all activity froze as if suspended in time. The newcomers drew all attention to their fearsome appearance. They imposed themselves with their arrogant strutting but in no favourable way; instinct warned me an ill wind had blown these men my way. Men of rank, I assumed, they were dressed in timber wolf fur leggings with shoulder pelts of the same animal draped over their woollen tunics, held in place by crossed leather straps. This assessment I affirmed by noting the detail of their costly wrought clasps.

If the impression they wished to make was of force and menace by their gait and scowling faces, it would have no effect on me. I had faced far worse in the shield-wall. My cringing servants irritated me but unreasonably – unlike me, they are minions, not warriors.

The canons of hospitality brought me to my feet.

"Welcome, travellers! Who are you and what is your purpose in the court of Heidaby?"

"Greetings, Lord Ulf," one drawled. I did not like his tone. "We are Bjørn Ingesson," he beat his chest with his fist and with the same hand indicated the man to his right. "Magnus Olavson," the hand swept out to include the strangers to his left, "Sigurd Steinarsson and Vidar Leifson. We are four *dispossessed* jarls from Skåne."

The manner in which he snarled the word alerted me to peril. Out of the corner of my eye, the slight movement of hands to hilts confirmed that my housecarls had also heeded it. I would not tolerate bloodshed in my hall – not before the infant playmates. My eyes must have followed my thoughts because Bjørn Ingesson's gaze stalked mine to settle on Sweyn and Harthacnut. Young and oblivious to all danger, they were rolling a patchwork cloth ball from one to the other across the floor.

"What have we here? One will be your boy, Lord Ulf, and the other Cnut's whelp. But which is which?"

"That is no concern of yours, stranger. Not until I learn the purpose of your visit."

With difficulty, I kept the hiss out of my voice. "For the moment, they are *both* my boys."

The forced laugh from the Swede did nothing to settle my jangling nerves and his next words endorsed my sensations.

"It is well you are cautious and hospitable, Lord Ulf, for our humour is not of the best."

"Guests are welcome within my walls, Bjørn Ingesson, as long as their conduct is befitting of the reception they are accorded."

"As to the purpose of our visit, *my Lord...*" what was the point in using a politeness if the tone did not match the gentility? "...our quarrel is not with you but with your King, who sits in splendour in England whilst removing the seats from under our arses."

"Speak clearly, lest regretful misunderstandings occur, son of Inge."

"What misunderstanding can there be, Lord Ulf? It is plain, as clear as the summer sky over Lund. King Cnut will spark off the greatest fire these lands have ever seen. In Skåne, he rides roughshod over generations of rights."

"Ay," the others chorused and nodded their agreement.

I sank down on my seat and with my body my heart too. This was what Eilaf had warned me about and I had done nothing.

"Tell me what is happening in Skåne."

Bjørn Ingesson made an exaggerated incredulous face and showed it to his three companions, who dutifully sniggered.

"Lord Ulf pretends he is ignorant of what is going on across the water. Are we to believe him?"

Again, they subserviently shook their heads.

"Take care, Bjørn Ingesson, do not imply I am a liar in my own hall. Know that I fear no man face to face."

A range of emotions crossed the scarred visage. Like myself, this man was no stranger to battle.

"Forgive my poor choice of words, Lord Ulf. All men tell of your worth in combat and of your reputation for honesty and fair-minded-ness – it is what brings us here."

At last, we were coming to the point. His placatory tone eased the tension threatening to lead my sword arm to stray.

"To what purpose, friend?"

"To explain our situation, claim redress and satisfaction."

"But how can I help if I do not understand? Speak your mind"

"*King* Cnut," he sneered the title, "advances like wildfire in Skåne. His Jarl, Arne, with his blessing, seizes property held by families for many lifetimes. Those who do not bend the knee are slain or driven into exile – like us. Soon, the whole of the country will be in his hands as far as the confines with Uppland. And who is to say where his land lust will end? Cnut has taken what is ours and we are come to take what is his."

Bjørn Ingesson's eyes roved to the two squabbling infants. His meaning was clear.

"I warn you, any attempt to seize the child will not finish well. You will not leave the building alive." My hand was now on my sword hilt. As I uttered these words came the sound of a score of steel blades leaving their scabbards around the sides of the hall.

"There is no immediate threat to you or yours, Lord. We come in peace on the advice of your brother to issue a warning."

My heart skipped. "Eilaf? What part has he in this?"

"He is concerned at Arne's menace to your family's estates in Upsal and is preparing for war. He sends word that you must look to Jutland, for that is where we are headed."

"Jutland?"

"The freemen meet regularly to decide what to do about Cnut. They are tired of their King's absence and worry he will impose himself on their lands as he has done in England and is now doing in Skåne. Do you see, we have a common cause?"

"I understand the injustice of what has happened to you, Bjørn Ingesson, but you must give me time to decide how to right the wrong. I am sworn to rule in the interests of the son of Cnut. The circumstances need much thought."

"There is, with respect, Lord, little time for thought. Action is what is needed – swift and decisive. Your brother sends word through us that King Olaf and King Anund Jacob have joined against Cnut. Olaf is in contact with the Jutland lords because he rejects Cnut's claim to his throne. The King of England searches for allies in Norway. He is offering gifts and treasure to local chiefs around Olaf's land with promises that they can have their old privileges back if they accept him as King. The chieftains smart under the yoke of Olaf's *hird* – his royal guard – who force them to obey all Olaf's laws." Bjørn swallowed hard and paused, his gaze meaningful, as if his detailed explanation had been of considerable importance.

"These chiefs welcome Cnut's offers, do they?"

"Of course, and there's more...Olaf is preparing to sail to Denmark. Lord Ulf, you will be forced to choose. Ponder well. Word has it that Thorkell the Tall and Cnut are reconciled. Nothing now keeps your wife-brother in England. He too prepares for war. Your safety and that of your ward are in the balance. You say we won't leave here alive and I see you are right." He glanced around at the bared blades, and his expression darkened, "We are not alone. The time will come very soon when you will have to take a stand. We wish that you are with us rather than against us. But choose you must."

Refusing to let his threats anger me, I replied calmly, "And so I will, Bjørn Ingesson, but my father taught me *'choose in haste and regret at length'* – I will not be hurried into a decision. Meanwhile, you are my guests. Join us at my table this evening, that our conversation might be of a more pleasant nature."

"I thank you Lord, but we must depart for Jutland because, as I said, time is pressing." He bowed and they took their leave, but not before the wretch bent and ruffled the hair of both children. The threat behind the gesture was so evident that ten of the nearest guards stepped forward and Bjorn hastened to straighten and stride towards the door. A raising and tilting of my head were sufficient to allow them to leave and for my housecarls to sheath their weapons.

Their visit plunged me into agonised thought. I had never warmed to Cnut, owing to the incident on Thanet after his father's death. His ambition threatened to turn the Baltic Sea blood red. Nonetheless, my sworn duty was to him to protect his four-winter's-old son, whom I loved. What I had told Bjørn Ingesson – they are both my boys – was not an untruth as far as my affections lay. Whatever position I chose to adopt, I must take the child's best interests into account. The threat to his well-being could not have been clearer. For sure, seizing Harthacnut as hostage would make the dispossessed lords' bargaining stance stronger.

My sympathies were with them, truth be told. I knew how I would feel, like Eilaf, if my home were snatched away by Cnut's desire to forge himself a northern empire. If I gave in to my heart, I would join the rebels in Jutland. In addition, King Olaf was of their part. To serve him would be natural for me. What would be unnatural would be to violate the principle by which I led my life – I eschewed treachery. I would rather lose my sword arm than go back on my bounden word. But what was it I had sworn: I would rule in the best interests of the minor, Harthacnut. Whether it would benefit the child to be seized and used as a hostage was not open to discussion. How to prevent it from happening most certainly was. I needed time to ponder the solution to this dilemma.

Bjørn Ingesson implied little or no time for deliberation. But if critical events were imminent, I would need to be sure of how to react. I jumped from my seat and called the leader of my housecarls.

"Helmer, I want those four men followed to Jutland. Send reliable spies after them. I must learn what they do and, above all, what they intend to do."

I strode to my chamber, threw myself on my bed and became immersed in deep thoughts. But often the plans we imagine are sound at the moment of conception take on another aspect in the face of events.

Estrid was surprised to find me in the chamber. Swollen with our second child in her womb, she waddled into the room.

"Husband, what are you doing abed at this hour?"

She is my consolation and I cannot keep secrets from her. It would be futile to try because it is as if she can read my mind. So it came as no surprise when she asked, "What ails you, my Lord?"

I explained the exchanges of the encounter. But as I did so, could not help but worry she would unhesitatingly take the part of her brother. I seldom underestimate Estrid but confess on this occasion I did her an injustice. Not only could she understand my awful predicament, but she could also see a way out of it.

"Ulf, dearest, you swore to act for the sake of Harthacnut. He is like a second son to us. You can't stand by and let the lords who are against my brother harm his interests nor can you do nothing at all while your King's actions are challenged..." I sighed and stared at the roof rafters. "...so, you must hasten to King Olaf and dissuade him from any action against us and Harthacnut."

"What if he commands me to hand over the boy or to fight on his side? And how can I leave you in your present state?"

"You can't consign Harthacnut but you can stand against Cnut if it's better for the boy. You will not be breaking your oath. In any case, by going to Olaf, you will learn his intentions."

"I employ spies for that. There's no need for me to move an inch."

"But you know how Olaf cares for you. What harm can it do to share your burden with him? Don't worry, the baby is not due for two moon cycles."

I wondered about listing the mischiefs that could come of it. But, not having a better plan and also respecting Estrid's judgement, I settled upon a visit to King Olaf. This fateful decision was helped by my worries over the strength of a Norwegian-Swedish alliance and by Eilaf's warning. If I could prevent war, I would do so but, above all I would work on behalf of Harthacnut.

21

THE ISLE OF KARMT, NORWAY, 1023 AD

B ear with me while I recount what I witnessed at the King's Hall in 1023 – an insight into Norway at the time. It will explain how difficult were dealings with King Olaf. This is the background to the events.

A man named Asbjorn Sigurdson, although baptised, continued his father's heathen practices when he inherited his rich farm at eighteen years of age. These involved feasting and sacrifices at harvest time, Yule and Easter with many people invited. Soon after taking over the farm, poor weather caused the corn harvests to fail. For the winter feast Asbjorn determined it should go ahead, and to make it possible, visited his friends, buying wheat from them wherever he could. In the spring, people had little seed for the ground and had to purchase the seed-corn. The summer of 1022 proved another bad year for grain. In addition to these difficulties, news came from the south that King Olaf prohibited all exports of grain, malt or meat to the northern parts of the country. This policy was part of his punitive campaign to stamp out heathenism in Norway and especially in the north, which he considered a breeding ground of paganism.

In the face of this intransigence, Asbjorn decided to put to sea in his long-ship and sailed southward to the island of Karmt where they stopped for the night. On the isle lived Thorer Sel, the King's bailiff, well-known for his inflexibility and for being high in Olaf's favour.

At first light, Thorer went down to the vessel with men and enquired about the owner and his business. Asbjorn presented himself and stated that he sought to purchase corn and malt as times were hard in the north.

"Farmer, will you sell us corn?" Asbjorn asked. "There are huge corn stacks and it would suit us not to travel on."

"You need to go no farther to buy grain, or journey in these provinces, because the King forbids carrying corn out of these lands to the north of the country. Sail back home, Halogalander, for it is the safest course for you."

Asbjorn glared and in a bold voice replied, "If there is no corn for us to buy, I will go forward with my errand and visit my relative, Erling."

"Where does he reside and what is he to you?"

"He is my mother's brother—"

"It may be I have spoken heedlessly if you are the sister's son of Erling. We wish you a good voyage, and come here again on your way back."

Asbjorn promised to do so and his men struck their tents before turning their ship to sea.

Happy to welcome his nephew, Erling asked how things were in the north. On hearing the grave news of his relatives' difficulties, he explained that the King had forbidden the sale of corn. "I know no man here who has the courage to break the King's command. For my part, Asbjorn, I find it difficult to keep well with the King, as so many foes are trying to break our friendship."

"As a child, my mother vaunted how she was freeborn throughout her whole descent and the boldest relative was Erling. Uncle, I now learn you do not have the freedom to do with your own grain as you please."

"You Halogalanders know less of the King's might than we do.

You may be bold in your speech back home. But come, let's drink and see what tomorrow brings."

After a merry evening, the next day Erling said, "Does it matter to you from whom you buy wheat?"

"All that matters is the price be fair."

"Well then," the older man smiled, "There is a way, Asbjorn. My slaves have as much grain as you require and they are not subject to law and land regulation like other men."

The slaves brought forward corn and malt, which they sold eagerly. With ten men, Asbjorn loaded his ship and left with presents from Erling and a kind farewell. A stiff wind sped him into Karmtsund, where they moored for the night.

There, Thorer Sel heard of Asbjorn's return and of his vessel deeply laden. Acting fast, Thorer gathered sixty armed men and at first light took them out to the Halogaland ship. Greeting the craft's owner, he asked Asbjorn what kind of merchandise his craft carried.

"Corn and malt."

"Then Erling is up to his usual tricks, despising the King's commands. He is tireless in opposing him in all things. I wonder the King suffers it."

Asbjorn explained Erling's slaves had owned the grain, and so no law was broken.

Not satisfied, Thorer replied, "Asbjorn, there is nought for it; either go ashore or we will throw you overboard because we will have no trouble while we unload your goods."

Without men enough to resist Thorer, the ship's owner reluctantly complied. To add an insult to the offence he had caused, after unloading all the cargo, Thorer made an unhappy decision and gave orders:

"Those Halogalanders have excellent sails – take the old sail off our vessel and give it to them! It is good enough for navigating with an unloaded vessel."

Seething with rage, Asbjorn swore one day he would avenge himself for this injury. Tales of his misfortune circulated and he found himself a laughing stock, which did not lessen his resentment towards Thorer Sel.

Then came Candlemas, when both Asbjorn and I, from far different places, put to sea and headed for King Olaf's court. I travelled with this intent, Asbjorn did not. He took ninety well-armed men aboard his ship. By Easter, they arrived at Karmt Island, where they landed in a deserted, uninhabited, part of the isle, and so their arrival went unobserved. He left his men in their tents to discover what was happening thereabouts. To this end, he put on poor clothes and a broad-brimmed hat, with a fork in hand, so he looked like a farm worker, but girded a sword under his garments.

At the same time I ordered our anchor to be dropped in the Karmtsund among many other vessels and upon gazing landwards, saw people flocking towards the hall built on a knoll. This was the sight Asbjorn spied and whereas to me, it seemed normal, because I knew of the King's presence here for Easter, to the Halogalander it seemed extraordinary.

I rowed ashore with five of my housecarls but Asbjorn went quietly to a house near the hall where servants were cooking meat. In a trice, he learned King Olaf had come to a Christian Easter feast and had just sat at table. I received the warmest welcome from my friend, the monarch, and a seat next to him was found for me as my rank as Regent of Denmark required.

At once Thorer Sel, our host, made himself known and presented me with an ornate drinking horn full to the brim with ale. Asbjorn headed to the hall and mingled with people coming and going in the ante-room where nobody took notice of him.

The hall-door was open and he saw Thorer Sel standing before the table of the high-seat.

Laughing, one of the jarls called upon their host to recount the tale of what had occurred between him and the Halogalander, Asbjorn.

Amid much merriment, Thorer gave a long account with much fabrication and embellishment all designed to diminish Asbjorn.

The same jarl asked mirthfully, "How did Asbjorn behave when you discharged his vessel?"

"When we were taking out the cargo he bore it like a man but when we took his sail from him, he wept like a babe."

This was met by gales of laughter and I must admit, it struck me as amusing too. Our gaiety was soon ended when a shabby figure burst into the room. It happened in the blink of an eye before anyone could react. Sword drawn, Asbjorn rushed into the hall and slashed at Thorer, cutting into the throat, so that slain, his body slumped across the table before King Olaf. The table turned slippery red.

"Seize this villain and take him from my sight!" the King cried.

My housecarls were the first upon him, pinning his arms and dragging him from the hall. Servants hastened to remove the table furniture and Thorer's corpse before wiping up all the blood. I have to say, King Olaf, although furious, to his credit remained quiet in his speech.

"A villain breaks the Easter peace, Lord Ulf, kills the host in the King's lodging and makes my table his execution block. Does this appear a small matter to you?"

Shocked by events I could not be expected to impart wisdom, so I shook my head and decided this was a bad time to talk about affairs in Denmark.

There are conflicting tales of what happened in the next few days. I know that in some way the islanders frustrated Olaf's will, determined to execute Asbjorn, who lay in irons. Finding excuses, they delayed the sentence. Having gained time, the prisoner's uncle arrived with a force of fifteen hundred men, intent upon paying the *mulct*, or wergild, in compensation for the death of Thorer Sel.

Outraged, King Olaf had no intention of commuting the verdict. I'm sure it was not that Asbjorn committed the crime under his horrified gaze at his table that offended Olaf, but that the assault happened during the holy peace of Easter. I stared anxiously into the Sound at the array of anchoring vessels.

"We do not have men enough to fight," the King echoed my

thoughts. "As well you are here for I shall require your counsel, Lord Ulf."

I smirked, "I came here to seek yours, my King."

Olaf clapped me on the back, "Then perhaps we can trade advice, my friend. But first, let us repair to the church for Mass."

Erling's company went straight to the house where his nephew lay in irons as the priest read to us from the Gospels. There they broke off his chains and at the tumult and clash of arms, the people of the village ran into the church for safety. I was among those who turned to stare at the interruption but King Olaf alone stood still, unmoved, without looking around him. Erling and his sons drew up their troops either side of the path leading from the church to the hall.

When Mass ended, King Olaf, with me, hand on sword hilt by his side, led the way unflinchingly between the rows of warriors until we reached the door of the hall. There Erling blocked the entrance so my hand itched to draw the weapon, whatever the odds against us, but the captive's uncle greeted Olaf courteously.

"My relation, Asbjorn, has been guilty of a misdemeanour, King. I received reports that it was a grave crime that incurs your displeasure. I am come to entreat peace for him and to pay those penalties such as you determine, but that redeem life and limb, and his permanence in his native land."

I caught my breath at these last words for they nullified at once the one counsel I had prepared for Olaf – namely, to banish Asbjorn to my court in Heidaby.

The King gave a level stare at the man blocking his way and with great calmness said:

"It seems with this display of force, Erling, you suppose the case of Asbjorn to be in your power. I fail to understand why you speak as though offering terms for him."

"Only you, Lord, may determine that we shall be reconciled."

"Did you think to frighten me with such numbers? If that is your thought, I will *not* turn and fly."

"My King, how many times have we met with me having fewer men than you had? Now, I will openly state it is my will that we enter into reconciliation otherwise we shall never meet again."

"Sire," I spoke almost in a whisper, "I entreat you to be reconciled with Erling according to his offer. Let the captive live sound in body, but then deal with him to your pleasure."

To my relief, Olaf said, "Erling, do you give security for Asbjorn, such as I think sufficient and then leave the conditions to my mercy, and all in my power?"

"Sire, name the surety, and I shall pay it willingly."

The matter was swiftly settled, whereupon Asbjorn received his safe passage, delivered himself under the King's authority, and kissed his hand. Erling withdrew his force and left the isle. Olaf led the way into the hall and I followed with Asbjorn beside me. I was curious as to what fate awaited him.

The King of Norway, however, was clement.

"Asbjorn, you must submit to that law which states the man who kills a servant of the King must undertake his service. I decree you will assume the office of bailiff which Thorer Sel held and manage my estate here."

This was agreed and as far as I knew, the matter ended there. It did not, but it was no longer my concern. I had other pressing issues on my mind.

The King then went on to lecture his new bailiff about how he would not tolerate the heathen practices of the Halogalanders on this isle. But Asbjorn was quick to reassure the King he was a baptised Christian, which of course was a half-truth that satisfied his monarch. For my part, I could not help but think the King's fervour for his religion brought about more problems than it solved. I determined that however heathen areas of Denmark might remain, I would leave them in peace to their soul-condemning ignorance.

Regarding Denmark I had to speak with the King, but decided to let the effects of recent events settle until evening when I would broach my situation. With this in mind, I went for a walk alone, in an attempt to summon my thoughts into some semblance of order for their later exposition to the King. The Isle of Karmt could not boast vast settlements, so I was surprised to come upon a foundry hidden in a dell. More surprising was the activity in its workshop as passing the door, I was drawn within out of curiosity. A man with a hammer and a letterform was inscribing the still damp loam mould in the form of a bell, known as the cope.

"Mind if I watch a man at his work?"

"Feel free, Lord."

Over his shoulder, I read the year -1024 in Latin numerals MXXIV and the words '*Olavum me fecit*'.

"Is the bell to be a gift of our King?" I asked.

"Did you not know, Lord? This beauty will go overseas for the Iceland people who have changed their laws and introduced Christianity, according to the word of our King. He sent timber for the building of a church to be built on their Thing-field and this will follow when we've done." He straightened from tapping in the last letter. "Will you stay to watch the casting? The copper and tin will be ready for I see they've skimmed off the slag."

I had never seen such an operation and readily said I would like to watch.

"Best to stand over there; dangerous material is molten bronze."

To his call, a young fellow hurried over and helped position the cope, with great care over the core mould. Both moulds were now clamped together so tightly that no bronze could flow out and be wasted or cause imperfection. I looked on as four men carried a ladle with a pouring lip in an ingenious device that permitted tilting. The care with which they walked was proof enough of the life-threatening danger of the molten metal.

Carefully positioning the ladle above the mould, they guided the lip above the hole predisposed to receive the flow. With a gentle tilt, a golden lava seethed forth and flowed into the gap between the moulds to form the bell. When they had finished I asked:

"How long before it's cool enough to break the mould?"

"Two days, Lord, but we'll give it three. Can't afford any slips. It's the first and probably the last bell to be made on this isle. Then we'll do the skirting."

"The what?"

"Skirting, it's the smoothing of any roughness at the rim of the bell."

I was impressed by what I'd seen and as I continued on my way, reflecting on the greatness of Olaf's mission. He had Christianised Norway, but not content had reached as far as Iceland and by all accounts had brought the Orkney Isles under his power. Word was that he had also made friendships in Greenland and the Farey islands. I had seen them drawn on a map in the King's chamber, otherwise they would have been mysterious names to me. I'd like to sail to Greenland one day. They tell me the whales are a wondrous sight.

Fresh sea air has always cleared my mind. It helps me sort out my thoughts whenever I have a problem. My path had taken me to the edge of a cliff. Gulls wheeled threateningly overhead and I thanked the Lord it was not springtime. Gulls become very aggressive in the breeding season if a man approached their nest. I knew of more than one man who lost an eye attempting to gather gulls' eggs which are a delicacy I too had enjoyed in the past. But I digress; my thoughts ought to have been fixed on my mission. What I had seen in the foundry confirmed my resolve to speak with King Olaf when I returned to the hall. I needed my powerful friend's support. Indeed, the bell-making I had witnessed would be a pleasing introduction to the King's ears before I entered upon my real purpose. So pleasing was it that he arranged for us to ride to the foundry in three days to observe the breaking of the mould and watch the skirting, so that we should be the first to hear the tone of the new bell.

"All will be well, Ulf. I had a master bell-maker brought over from Heidaby. The foundry workers here had never made a bell, you know?"

"He will be the man who was inscribing the mould with your name, Sire. He knew what he was doing."

Most serious politics are conducted at a table in my experience, and on this agreeable occasion King Olaf consented to ignore any invitations to warlike involvement in Jutland. In return, he had my solemn promise that Denmark would not make any attempt to seize Norwegian territory. The monarch was quite open about his improved relationship with Sweden and pointed out that the biggest threat to the Baltic was Cnut and what was taking place in Skåne. Our agreement would be binding, he stressed, as long as Cnut did nothing to upset it.

This caveat, however, I was well aware might throw more than our understanding to the greedy ravens.

22

HEIDABY 1024 - 1026 AD

I left the Jutland freemen with assurances of non-belligerence from Norway, and from me in return receiving promises of allegiance to Cnut. There was no hint of the trouble to come; not that I departed convinced of their trustworthiness – far from it. Their eyes did not share their smiles and reassurances.

My visit to Olaf served to gain respite, a blessing given my family situation. Estrid gave birth to a healthy babe soon after my return to Heidaby – our second son, Bjørn. His name is 'bear' in our language as I wished to honour my ancestor's ursine origins. There would come a day, God willing, when Bjørn's grip will crush a hand but for the moment it curled gently around my forefinger.

I remember those weeks of calm, shared with my wife and children as the happiest of my life. But they proved to be the quiet before the storm. The first heavy rain came in the form of aggression from the Jutland lords I had encountered on their home soil. They strode into my hall as if they were the rightful owners with their threats and bluster. I had been warned by my lookouts of their imminent arrival and expected them to be bristling with weapons. They did not disappoint, but I wore my chainmail over-shirt. They found me with my feet planted well apart in the centre of the room, battleaxe at the ready.

"Lord Ulf," one of the scoundrels took the lead, glancing uneasily at the well-armed housecarls lining the walls, "you look as if you are expecting trouble."

"The only trouble I'm anticipating is the labour awaiting my servants when they have to mop your blood from my floor."

"What kind of a welcome is that?"

"One befitting those who come armed and uninvited into my home. Unless you have ought worthwhile to impart, I bid you leave my hearth at once or suffer the consequences..."

I believe I was spoiling for a fight as these Jutlanders were not to my taste.

"Be not so hasty, Lord Ulf, lest your words presage sluggish regret. We are only a few envoys but speak for all our people."

I glared at the villain with the close-set eyes disappearing in the blue painted band running menacingly from ear to ear.

"Then I can but hope your populace sends you with a less rude message than your chosen method of delivering it."

"Enough of fancy words, we come to warn that the loyalty we promised to Cnut and his son Harthacnut no longer holds."

"Why break your given word?"

I swung my axe with the slightest movement by my leg, enough to catch his eye but not to alarm him into rashness.

Seeing him grow pale at the threat pleased me, but I wanted to be rid of them by fair means or otherwise. At the same time, I wished to know what was amiss to provoke the intrusion.

"Because King Cnut has unleashed his hounds on Skåne and tramples the birthright of the Skånians underfoot. Cnut is also a Christian and imposes his religion on those under his yoke. We will have none of this."

"Do you think to defy your rightful King? Can you not see such an act will provoke him into gathering a vast fleet and sailing to Jutland at once? Is not Christianity spreading throughout the northern lands and already established in Europe? Do you think you can resist the tide and make it turn at your command? I think not. I will have no more treasonable talk in my hall. Do not fan the flames of my ire."

"You have not yet heard our terms."

"Do you suppose to dictate conditions from a position of weakness? If so, you Jutlanders are more stupid than your appearance."

They shuffled uncomfortably and the one with flashing eyes thrust the speaker aside:

"Thus far, we are led by Loge," and he indicated the crestfallen spokesman, "but I believe a more wary and respectful way of talking will suit."

"Go on, then."

Encouraged by my consent, this younger, wiser and more muscular fellow said, "We were charged with a caution, Lord. It is true what Loge said; the men of Jutland are alarmed at what they hear from Skåne and will not suffer similar abuses. Denmark lacks a firm leadership with its King far away in England but from what we see, his reach is long and unjust."

"What, then, is the warning?"

I tapped my axe-head against my leg in an unmistakable gesture of annoyance. It drove him to gabble his admonition.

"If there is no change in the present situation, the men of Jutland will choose their own King."

"Will they indeed? And risk the wrath of King Cnut and of the Regent of Denmark who acts in the interests of his monarch's son? Ought I to thank you for coming and issuing your warnings? But remember this: you cannot unblow a horn any more than you can unring a bell. It tells me how things stand with you and that I should raise an army to meet you in the field."

"It need not come to that, Lord Ulf. We are looking to you to find a peaceful solution."

"What with your battleaxes and swords at the ready?"

"We feared we might have to protect ourselves."

179

"Very prudent, under the circumstances."

How long this pointless exchange might have continued I'll never know because I lost patience and ordered them out of the hall. My housecarls, as one, unsheathed their swords and advanced on the Jutlanders, ushering them out like frightened sheep before so many wolves.

With hindsight I should have moved, there and then, with the decisiveness of King Olaf in Norway when under threat. It is to my regret that I was gripped by indecision. Instead of raising a force and marching into Jutland, I let the weeks drift by and allowed events to take control. Had I been less passive my tale might have had a different ending, but as they say, 'no use dwelling on spilt mead.'

I must be careful how I explain what happened because I do not wish posterity to believe the calumny that I betrayed King Cnut. I will admit to secret correspondence with his queen, Emma. But what was I, as Regent, supposed to do? I could not ignore the natural concerns of a mother cruelly separated from her son. I defy anyone to define the contents of our letters as treasonable. Unless of course, my actions in the best interests of Harthacnut could be interpreted as going against those of Cnut.

The growth of discontent in Jutland in 1025 became unstoppable and erupted in a series of rebellious moots. I was forced to raise an army and penetrate as far as Viborg. There, a delegation of dissidents, containing the familiar faces of my Heidaby intruders, presented themselves under a white flag. Hostile as ever the gist of their grievances had not changed, but the key point was the threat of war if they were not satisfied. I tasked myself to prevent this extreme solution: the main grievance could no longer be avoided – their resentment at being poorly served by an absentee King. Pressing also was the need to quell fears at Cnut's alleged menace to their liberties.

At Viborg, I took the fateful decision. I confess also to having constant contact with King Olaf, which might not have been my wisest policy. Queen Emma pressed me to enlist his support to sustain her son and since I considered Olaf my friend, I was tempted. As a result, the Norwegians prepared to invade Jutland by gathering a vast fleet in Throndhjem Fjord. Thence, the King sailed south, assembling more ships until his vessels numbered four hundred and eighty.

When word of this portentous happening reached me, for the first time the magnitude of my intervention struck me and made me vacillate. How could I condone a Norwegian invasion of the land I was charged to protect? My hesitation led to Olaf keeping his restless warriors in idle boredom. I risked alienating my long-term friend and destroying our relationship. His solution was to dismiss all but sixty ships, which he took to Skåne. Unbeknown to me, Olaf was in constant contact with the King of Sweden, both being concerned at Cnut's policy of expansion in the Baltic.

How much of what followed was my fault and how much due to Cnut's ambition or Queen Emma's treason, posterity will judge. I acted in good faith and upon receiving a letter with the King's signet. Unbeknown to him and to me, she had got hold of it and concealed it from him. When I met with the Jutland rebels, according to the will expressed in the letter, I declared the eight-year-old Harthacnut King of Denmark. Had I not done so at that particular time, I am convinced that in the absence of Olaf's support we would have been overwhelmed and slaughtered.

Can anyone say in all honesty that I betrayed Cnut by having the Jutlanders swear allegiance to the boy? Some say I acted out of personal ambition and in so doing I became the *de facto* ruler of Denmark. Who in their right mind would have wanted *that* kingdom in its current situation? I deny all accusations but aver to having saved Harthacnut's life, which was my bounden duty.

In Skåne a lord faithful to Cnut, named Hakon, fled to England with news of events in the region. In so doing, he gained a reward of prestigious estates in Skåne from his grateful King. His news provoked Cnut into raising a mighty fleet of splendid blue- red- and green-striped sails directed to Denmark.

At the awesome sight of this naval force, I ordered my small army to retreat inland.

"Harthacnut," I said, "God knows I have always treated you as a son and acted for your benefit. Hark, boy, you must now act like your own man, for you are in great peril. I am ashamed to say my well-meaning actions are to blame. By having you declared King of Denmark, I made you usurp your father's position. He is determined to take back his throne. You must throw yourself on his mercy. Tell him you love him and acted on my counsel."

The boy, due credit to him, had more about him than I believed.

"But what of you, Uncle Ulf? I will not do anything to cause you harm."

His eyes filled with tears. Who would have imagined such affection for me?

"Do not worry about me, Lord. The safest thing for me will be if you kneel before your father and submit to him."

In those weeks when my every decision proved flawed, at least this one was sound. Harthacnut hastened to meet his father in his encampment. At the sight of his son prostrate before him and begging his mercy, Cnut took him to be a witless youth I had manipulated. My circumstances were not helped by the instant capitulation of the Jutland rebels who bent the knee before their potent sovereign. In so doing, they undermined my argument of how perilous the Danish situation had become.

All I could do at this point was to run so I fled to join Eilaf in Skåne. I did not wish to fight my King and instead sent my son, Sweyn, to him to pray for grace and reconciliation with me. Sweyn offered himself as hostage on my behalf. When I sent men to offer terms, the cold reply was to collect forces and co-operate in the defence of the kingdom and that I might later make my proposals.

"Ulf, you must not listen to Cnut," Eilaf warned me, "even now he is heading to Skåne with the serpent Hakon who has betrayed us. You cannot trust Cnut – he is vindictive. Your life is not worth a burnt-down candle. You are a Swede and King Amond is my friend.

We must defend our father's estates. And hark! King Amond has allied with your mentor King Olaf. It is clear to me where your loyalties lie."

I stared into the handsome countenance of my brother and wavered.

"It may be clear to you, Eilaf, but Cnut is my wife-brother. I have left my wife and children in Heidaby – are these not stronger loyalties?"

"Send for Estrid and my nephews. They will be safe in Upsal. Think of our mother and home. Are they not worth fighting for?"

There was no answer to such reasoning. Of course, my prime loyalty must be to my origins. But my father's words tormented my mind as if he were alive and whispering in my ear: *Swear you will eschew treachery all your lives.* I had, after all, sworn allegiance to Cnut, by telling him in Winchester he could count on me.

"Eilaf, Cnut is our King. He raised you to Earl in England. Are we to betray him?"

"Open your eyes, Ulf. You are no longer the youth who swore an oath to keep father happy. You are a man now, with *three* Kings! You must, whatever happens, betray at least one of them. There is only one, at this moment, who wishes you dead."

In the face of such indisputable reasoning and the sincere concern on the countenance of my brother, who undoubtedly had been forced to make his own difficult choices, I surrendered.

There, on the wide beach of Halland's Weather Island, with stately beech trees of the forest swaying at our backs, I made another bad decision. Perhaps it was the beauty of my surroundings, my homeland, that swayed me. I would fight alongside my brother to destroy Cnut's imperial dream.

23

ZEALAND, MICHAELMAS, 1026 AD

I decided against sending Estrid and the children to Upsal. Should Cnut arrive in Heidaby I could not imagine him harming his sister and nephews, however great his wrath towards me. Instead, what guarantee was there that the young Swedish King, Anund Jacob, would not take them as hostages for his dealings with Cnut?

"You might have a point there, Ulf," Eilaf heeded my argument. Thus, we sailed to join the King of Norway off the coast of Zealand. When we arrived in our two long-ships, Olaf was ashore and we joined him. He had called a public moot with the idea of winning the Danes to his allegiance. Impressed by his eloquence, I feel sure the majority of listeners were swayed to his will. Sadly for Olaf, at this point, spies rushed to him warning they had seen ships approaching. An aged Dane stood, "Pay no heed, Sire, for they are only merchantmen."

Looking out toward the horizon, sails in great numbers began to appear.

The same greybeard rose, "Sire, it seems they are merchantmen come to buy Denmark with iron."

There was no choice but to return to our ships in the face of

Cnut's greater force. Our only option was to sail eastwards and attempt to unite with King Anund's fleet, occupied with harassing the Skånian coast.

Astern, Cnut's multi-coloured sails billowed in hot pursuit. We found some of Anund's vessels near Stangeberg, but far too few to resist the might of Cnut. King Olaf decided to sail on while the Swedes preferred to stay and fight. Eilaf was of the same mind. I could not bring myself to revolt against my wife-brother but did not wish to abandon my blood-brother.

"Eilaf, I pray you, do not rush into pointless conflict. You will be more useful to our cause alive."

"Ulf, I have never known you to be timid in the face of the enemy."

I glared at my brother.

"Two things, Eilaf: first, are you so sure that Cnut is our foe? And second, never again call me a coward if you value your hide. I am urging prudence and reflection."

My uncharacteristic hesitation served to take matters out of my hands. The one-sided engagement began with our long-ships standing off from where we understood the futility of heading into useless slaughter.

I signalled to Eilaf's ship.

"Come eastwards after Olaf, while we can!" I shouted. To my relief, his long-ship turned and set sail, the black raven followed our lead.

We found Anund and Olaf's ships east at the estuary of the River Helgeå, known as the Holy River. It is a short stream, an outlet for a group of lakes among dense forests. Anund's vessels were drawn up in battle order, so our craft sailed to join them. I did not. It was at this point that my conscience dominated my thinking. How could I fight my wife's brother who had entrusted Denmark to me? I had been foolish to follow the advice of my sibling who had not always wished me well. Fighting Cnut now would mean fighting against Harthacnut's inheritance and he was like a son to me.

185

I ordered a course westwards and intercepted Cnut's fleet. The King received me with cold suspicion, and who could blame him?

"Lord, I am come to fight by your side and to advise of what awaits you at the Holy River mouth."

The telling was rapid as was the reply.

"Welcome, Ulf, you will lead my fleet against the enemy."

Whether by setting me in the van of the attack Cnut was hoping to rid himself of me, or whether he believed I was best equipped for the role, I do not know.

This mattered less than other events I was ignorant of. It transpired that King Anund remained in charge of the fleet while Olaf went inland to prepare a trap at the lake out of which the River Helga flows. There at the riverhead they made a dam of timber and turf and also dug a deep ditch, through which he made flow several waters, so that the lake water grew very high. In the riverbed they positioned large logs of timber. This work took some days to complete.

By the time we arrived and saw the enemy craft lined up, it was twilight – too late for an engagement. Considering they also had the advantage of a carefully chosen position, I refused battle that day. Since the harbour at the river mouth was empty, I ordered as many ships to moor there as could be accommodated – another bad decision. The remainder I anchored outside near to the port.

It was natural that many of our force landed, conversed and sought amusement. At first light Olaf broke the dam, releasing the water into the course with the large tree trunks. The effect was devastating. Without warning a wall of water swept down in a raging torrent, drowning many of our men, both on land and on board ship. Hurtling timber slammed into our moored vessels, nearly capsizing them, incurring considerable damage and throwing men overboard to death by drowning.

"Quick, cut the ropes!" I cried. "They dammed the river!"

Those who could do so allowed their ships to drift and saved themselves. To my relief, King Cnut's great dragon was among these. I counted ten ships lost.

"Beware, Lord!" I bellowed seeing his oars could not manage to halt the drifting towards the hostile fleet. "Man the oars!" I yelled at my men and headed with all haste to succour the King. I waved and shouted to our other ships to join us because Cnut's vessel was surrounded. We drew near to aid the dragon-ship, so large that it had sixty banks of rowers, and the figurehead was gilt all over. So great was his ship, high like a castle, that they could not easily overcome it. On board, the carefully armed and well-trained warriors gave a splendid account of themselves. When we pitched in from all sides, unleashing a hail of death, the two Kings knew they faced defeat. Satisfied with the devastation they had inflicted, they turned and fled. With our own heavy losses, it was pointless to pursue an enemy who had suffered only slightly. This costly victory proved to be a turning point, leaving Cnut dominant in the Baltic. It also left me in an ambiguous position with regard to Cnut.

The King ordered us to sail back along the coast of Zealand and down the long fjord leading to the ancient settlement of Roskilde. The town was founded a lifetime ago by Harald Bluetooth and strangely, despite its importance, I had never set foot there. There is always a first – and a last - time. As we sailed into the harbour, as if by fate, the wooden Church of the Holy Trinity on the hill high above us caught my eye. An involuntary shiver ran down my spine.

In the bustle of men disembarking, Cnut sought me out. They led me to him, where I found him talking to my brother. I took this as a good sign. The King had clearly forgiven Eilaf for standing against him. I cast my mind back to Thorkell the Tall. Hadn't he also pardoned the Viking of Jómsborg? Was the situation as bleak as I feared?

"Come, Ulf," Cnut smiled, "you will know the royal palace stands near yonder church. It is there we must hie to feast and exchange tales of our victory."

I knew nothing of any residence but was heartened by Cnut's words. He seemed to bear me no grudge. I remained uneasy because I knew his vindictive nature only too well.

Feasting at the table, this unease grew as we discussed the events as custom required and the King began to ask pointed questions about what had led to the battle. His cold eyes bored into mine and I found, increasingly, I had to justify my stance by constant repetition of having acted in the interests of Harthacnut. That he did not believe me became plain. When he engaged in whisperings with his housecarls while his narrowed eyes never left my face, his hostility waxed as a certainty.

When men take strong drink and relax in feasting after a battle, at times tempers rise and injudicious words spring to the lips. Hoping to avoid this and knowing the King's love of certain pastimes, in an attempt to restore his good humour I accepted his challenge to me for a game of chess.

Cnut is such a skilful player that it must have been fate that provoked his wrong move and led me to take his knight. He glared across the table and I was shocked at the malice in that look. He moved my piece back and replaced his knight.

"Make another play, Lord Ulf."

What possessed me to overturn the board and leave the table, no-one will ever know.

"Are you running away now, timid Wolf?"

The scorn in his voice and the laughter of the assembly made me flush and reply, abandoning caution.

"Farther you would have run at the Holy River had you been able. You did not then call Ulf timid when I rushed to your aid while the Swedes were thrashing your men like dogs."

With these proud, unwise words fuelled by drink, I left the hall and took to my sleeping quarters.

Whether it was my imagination in a fever, whatever, I could not rest for I feared the malevolence of Cnut. The night drew on amid my tossing and turning. How many times I strained my ears to the slightest sound I lost count. At last I rose, for sleep would not come. I should have pulled on my mail coat but tiredness and a desire not to be perceived as belligerent prevailed. I believe destiny led me to the Church of the Holy Trinity.

I was convinced that Cnut would have me dead. I needed the quiet and solace of the church to clear my thoughts and take the many decisions that would return me safely to Estrid. That is why I went unarmed before the altar to kneel and pray. My vulnerability was emphasised by an eerie atmosphere created by the flickering candlelight, and lengthening dancing shadows restricted to small pools of light surrounded by impenetrable darkness.

In my experience, the sepulchral silence of a church is the best place to ponder. I began to reflect on the events that had shaped my life and led me here. Inevitably, my thoughts strayed to my father and his counsel: *'the root of your unhappiness is you desire to be loyal to your leader but you do not wish to serve what is petty and vile'*. I kept coming back to one concept – betrayal. I despise hypocrisy in all its forms but now I had to face a grave question. Had the honesty so critical to my morality proved to be a remedy far worse than the disease of betrayal it was called upon to cure? What is worse than acting out of a sense of duty when your heart pulls in another direction? I had striven to steer a righteous course but my ship had run aground and wrecked on the unforgiving, destructive, rocky shore of ambition and politics. Defeated, I sighed heavily when a footfall made me turn.

It was by now near dawn. The first glimmerings of daylight filtered weakly through the high windows to augment the candle-light. It gave enough light to see before me, sword in hand, the form of the Norseman Ivar White, Cnut's housecarl and nephew to Earl Eric, his eyes half-closed and hard. There would be no reverential awe of the sacrament in the soul of this half-heathen sworn enemy of King Olaf to save me. My doom had stridden in, glaring at me, defenceless, within the House of God.

"Sacrilege!" I murmured.

The word served to sting the reprobate into action. He took two steps towards me then hesitated. Had he lost the courage to finish me? Did he wish to take me alive for I know not what purpose? He breathed deeply, his gaze fixed, never wavering, on mine. Out came his seax from his belt while he raised his sword in the other hand. With a terrible guttural cry he lunged forward, and through my dying eyes I looked up at the bloodied blade.

So Cnut had forgiven Eilaf but could not find the grace to pardon his wife-brother, whose noble vision of a Nordic brotherhood contrasted and threatened to thwart his own dreams of imperial greatness. In the end, my rigidity had cost me dear.

My last thoughts were for Estrid and the boys, I could feel her love knot pendant pressed into my chest under my body on the floor. I would never embrace her again, nor live to see my dearest wish - Sweyn becoming a warrior. My failing sight observed the blood pooling in rivulets on the floor – the price of betrayal – flowing to the extinction of Ulf's Tale.

THE END

HISTORICAL NOTE

I would like to stress that *Ulf's Tale* is a work of historical fiction. While the majority of characters in the novel, including Jarl Ulf Thorgilsson, are historically documented, there is no solid evidence he possessed land in Norway or that he was an intimate counsellor of King Olaf. Otherwise, most of the events narrated are accurate but since primary sources are scarce, historians, with considerable caution, have to lean on the various Scandinavian sagas, such as the *Heimskringla*, which I drew upon for this tale.

Apart from an interest in late-Viking history, the inspiration for this story came from amazement at the importance of betrayal (the theme of the novel) in the events of eleventh-century Anglo-Scandinavian history. A conviction grew in my mind that Jarl Ulf, rather than being the traitor Cnut believed him to be, was rather a victim of his own morality. There were many treacherous turncoats in this period but I felt an empathy for Ulf. History can be strange in its assessments. Cnut was vindictive and murderous but has gone down as King Cnut the Great. I underline here that the idea of Ulf's motivations is my own and some historians will probably leap into their Spitfires and shoot me down but I write for the fun of it! I hope you agree and have enjoyed *Ulf's Tale*.

ABOUT THE AUTHOR

I was born in Cleethorpes Lincolnshire UK in 1948: just one of the post-war baby boom. After attending grammar school and studying to the sound of Bob Dylan I went to Nottingham University and studied Medieval and Modern History (Archaeology subsidiary). The subsidiary course led to one of my greatest academic achievements: tipping the soil content of a wheelbarrow from the summit of a spoil heap on an old lady hobbling past our dig. Well, I have actually done many different jobs while living in Radcliffe-on-Trent, Leamington, Glossop, the Scilly Isles, Puglia and Calabria. They include teaching English and History, managing a Day Care Centre, being a Director of a Trade Institute and teaching university students English. I even tried being a fisherman and a flower picker when I was on St. Agnes, Scilly. I have lived in Calabria since 1992 where I settled into a long-term job, for once, at the University of Calabria teaching English. No doubt my lovely Calabrian wife Maria stopped me being restless. My two kids are grown up now, but I wrote books for them when they were little. Hamish Hamilton and then Thomas Nelson published 6 of these in England in the 1980s. They are now out of print. I'm a granddad now and happily his parents wisely named my grandson Dylan. I decided to take up writing again late in my career. You know, when you are teaching and working as a translator you don't really have time for writing. As soon as I stopped the translation work I resumed writing in 2014. The fruit of that decision is my first historical novel, *Die for a Dove*, an archaeological thriller, followed by *The Purple Thread* and *Wyrd of the Wolf*, published by Endeavour Press,

London. Both are set in my favourite Anglo-Saxon period. Currently my third and fourth novels are available too, *Saints and Sinners* and its sequel *Mixed Blessings* set on the cusp of the eighth century in Mercia and Lindsey. A fifth *Sward and Sword* will be published in June 2019 About the great Earl Godwine. At the end of April, 2019 *Perfecta Saxonia* is published by Creativia and the same publishers will release *Ulf's Tale* at the beginning of May, 2019. Successively they will publish *Angenga*, a tale of time travel and *In the Name of the Mother*, the sequel to *Wyrd of the Wolf*. I'm now writing a ghost story, with Anglo-Saxon connections, of course!

Lightning Source UK Ltd.
Milton Keynes UK
UKHW010724110920
369747UK00001B/120